THE FINAL CURTAIN CALL

A Northwest Cozy Mystery - Book 11

BY

DIANNE HARMAN

Published by: Dianne Harman
www.dianneharman.com

Interior, cover design and website by
Vivek Rajan

ISBN: 9781696097734

CONTENTS

ACKNOWLEDGMENTS

This series started out because of my numerous trips to the Northwest to visit my son and his wife. I love the area and during one of my trips, came up with the basic idea for the Northwest Cozy Mystery Series.

Because of you, my readers, it has become my bestselling series. I'm so glad you like the characters and the ambiance of the area as much as I do. And I have to admit that I completely understand why so many people have written to tell me that Al DeDuco is their favorite character, of not only this series, but my others as well.

After all, you just have to root for an ex-Mafia man! There are a number of sayings based on this one: "You can take man out of..., but you can't take the... out of the man." To add one more saying, "You can take the man out of the Mafia, but you can't take the Mafia out of the man." And so my thanks to Al, for being such a wonderful character.

To the many people on my support team who work tirelessly on editing, creating book covers, looking for mistakes, and generally giving me advice, thank you!

And to Tom, who takes care of everything, so I can play the author role, thank you!

And to Kelly, my boxer dog, who lets me know by putting a paw in my lap, that it's time for me to get up from the computer and throw the ball for a few minutes!

And to all of you, thanks for taking your valuable time to read what I write!

Win FREE Paperbacks every week!

Go to www.dianneharman.com/freepaperback.html and get your FREE copies of Dianne's books and favorite recipes immediately by signing up for her newsletter.

Once you've signed up for her newsletter you're eligible to win three paperbacks. One lucky winner is picked every week. Hurry before the offer ends!

PROLOGUE

"No, Julius!" Angel Bridges said, tears pouring down her cheeks, her voice heaving, her hand shaking as she held the phone to her ear. "I want to do this. I want to use my voice. For far too long, I've been exclusively in front of the cameras, but I never wanted to be. Well, I did at the time, but it's not my passion. Opera is my passion, and always will be!"

She was standing on the balcony of the exclusive apartment director Tobias Crank had rented while he was in town putting on the opera *Akhnaten*. It afforded a wonderful view of Seattle at night, the skyscrapers all lit up, and making the vehicles below look like little fireflies as they moved in the darkness.

But Angel Bridges wasn't able to see the beauty in it. Why couldn't her husband understand what she was telling him?

"You know the only reason you want to do this opera is because of Tobias," Julius sneered on the other end of the line.

"No, Julius, that's not it at all." Angel cried. "You know it's you I love. Only you."

"Then prove it," Julius said. "Quit the opera."

"I can't do that," Angel said. "Tonight was opening night. People bought tickets to the opera because they've seen me in movies. I'm introducing a whole new audience of people to the opera."

Julius chuckled. "Okay, then, dear." He spoke with the kind of amused dismissal one gives to a little child, telling her she was going to be Queen of the World one day.

"Julius, please don't do this," Angel pleaded. She was talking through tears. "Why can't you just support me?"

"It's beyond me why you'd choose to be paid almost nothing to swan run around a stage singing in languages nobody understands," Julius said. His voice was light and playful, but the daggers in his intentions were real. And they were making Angel bleed.

"I know everyone doesn't appreciate opera, Julius, but…"

"You should have taken another movie role and gotten a decent paycheck."

"It's not all about money," Angel said desperately.

"Oh, isn't it?" he said, icily calm. "Well, then, why did you marry me? I'm not exactly a church mouse, am I?"

In fact, Julius was an extremely wealthy hedge fund manager, easily earning over $1,000,000 a year in his salary alone, and then there were the bonuses. He worked in California, where they both lived.

"I married you because I loved you," Angel said.

"If you loved me, you wouldn't have left me to go away to put on a nothing little opera."

"Julius, we both know I've been gone many times before for movies," Angel said. "You never said anything when I was gone then."

"No, I didn't, because I knew it was worth it. I knew we'd have money in the bank and a movie to show for it. But this? Really, Angel, I know you've made some poor choices in your past, but I thought you'd matured beyond that by now."

"Poor choices," Angel repeated, feeling numb. He was talking about her previous marriage. She'd married a fellow actor, who had turned out to be physically abusive, and she'd left him. For some reason, Julius always saw this as a fault to hold over her, both her marrying the actor, and then leaving him, which to Julius meant disloyalty.

In fact, pretty much anything Angel did Julius could twist into something negative. Angel's family and friends despaired at her relationships with men. She was truly an exceptional woman. She was extraordinarily talented, beautiful, richer than most people's wildest dreams, stylish, charming, and kind.

But for some reason that no one knew, not even Angel, she seemed to be a magnet for men who wanted to bring her down, rather than celebrate her.

Angel's head was spinning. That always seemed to be Julius' effect on her. As she was trying to formulate a response, she heard the door behind her open.

She turned and looked at someone who had just stepped out on the balcony. "Oh, it's you," she said, then quickly muted the phone. Julius always asked so many questions if he heard her talking to anyone when they were on the phone.

"I heard you crying," the person said, "and I thought I'd bring you a drink. Don't lose sight of why we're here tonight, to celebrate our fantastic opening night. You were absolutely spectacular."

"Thank you," Angel said, then nodded at her phone, indicating she was on a call. She took the glass of champagne offered her, and turned again to look over Seattle's skyline and try to get her head together. She unmuted the call after the person who had brought her the champagne stepped back inside the apartment. "Babe, I'm here."

"Who was that?" he asked icily.

"No one. No one."

"You muted me. Was it Tobias Crank?"

"No!"

"It was Tobias Crank, wasn't it? That so-called director. Was he talking about how you're going to get between his sheets later, hey?"

"It wasn't anyone," Angel said desperately. "I promise. It was… a waiter. Bringing me some champagne."

"You can't lie to me, Angel. I can read your mind."

"No, you can't," Angel said, but she was unsure and scared. Sometimes it really did feel like he could look into her thoughts. She was beginning to feel a little dizzy.

"Anyway, who cares who it was… Let's say it was Tobias Crank, and you're having your fun up in Seattle. I can just as easily have my fun here in California, Angel. Plenty of girls here are up for a good time."

"No, Julius, please don't."

He chuckled. "Please, what?"

"Please don't cheat on me," she said, feeling broken. "Please. I promise, nothing is going on. I swear it."

"Swear on your life?"

"I swear. I swear it, babe. It's you I love. Only you."

"You'd better be telling the truth," he said. "I had a good friend whose wife was cheating on him. She swore on her life she wasn't, then she was diagnosed with Stage four ovarian cancer a couple of months later. I'd hate for something like that to happen to you."

Angel gulped. "That won't happen to me," she said, "because I'm telling the truth. I always tell you the truth. You're my husband." Her head was starting to hurt.

"All right," he said, softening a little. "And you're my lovely wife. I'm sorry, babe. You can't get mad at a man because he gets a little paranoid now and then. Especially when he's got such a beautiful, gorgeous wife that any man would want to steal away."

Angel breathed a sigh of relief. He was back to "normal," though moments of him being nice were becoming rarer and rarer these days. She was going to tell him how much she loved him, but she had a sudden wave of nausea, and her dizziness was beginning to make the Seattle skyline spin horribly. "Babe... I don't feel well."

"Oh dear," he said sweetly. "Maybe you should go home from the party. After all, there are only horrible people there who want..."

But Angel Bridges didn't hear the rest of what her husband said, because she had dropped to the floor, unable to breathe. Her phone clattered down on the tile next to her and the screen smashed.

"Jullllius!" she said, wheezing. The whole world was closing in on her and her vision had blacked out.

In less than a minute, she was dead.

CHAPTER ONE

"It's good to be back," DeeDee said, looking up at Seattle's most prestigious apartment building. "And we have a great client to kickstart my return. I must say, Susie, you've done an incredible job on the marketing to pull in such a client."

Susie beamed as they went through the glass revolving doors into the bright, shining lobby, complete with a marble floor. "Thanks, DeeDee," she said. "I wasn't sure about putting the ad in the most exclusive magazine in Seattle. It cost a lot, and I mean a lot."

"That was a brave move," DeeDee said. "But it certainly seems to have paid off." She looked around at the fountain and expensive paintings in the lobby and said again, "and I mean, paid off."

DeeDee and her husband, Jake, had been in Connecticut to take over a friend's private investigation firm when he needed to be with his wife in her struggle to overcome cancer.

Jake had left his private investigating firm in Seattle in the hands of their good friend Al DeDuco, a former member of the Mafia who had gone straight and married DeeDee's friend Cassie, a prominent restaurant critic. Al had to fake his own death when some Mafia members came after him, reminding him that with the mob, the past never stays in the past.

He, Cassie, DeeDee, and Jake had rushed to Chicago to put things to rest. Thankfully, since then everything had been quiet, and Al hadn't had any more death threats. It looked like the chapter in his new life was finally in full swing and no old loose threads from the past could come and interrupt the story.

After signing in with the receptionist and getting visitor passes, they rode up in the large, mirrored elevator to the 10th floor, where their client, Tobias Crank, was staying.

"I've never much been into opera," DeeDee said. "If I had to choose, I'd prefer to go to a musical. At least then I could understand what was going on."

Susie grinned. "Me, too. Paragons of culture, aren't we?"

DeeDee flashed her a smile. "Perhaps we'll learn to love it, since we'll be around all these opera types. I wonder if we'll be invited to the opera."

"Well, the guy sounded pretty friendly on the phone," Susie said. "You never know."

"We need to pretend to like opera very much," DeeDee said with a laugh. "Otherwise he might be offended. I like the fact you spoke to the man himself, though, not an assistant. Maybe that means he's approachable and down to earth."

Tobias Crank was very friendly, they discovered, and extremely approachable. But down to earth? Not in the slightest, and they realized that the moment they stepped through the door of his apartment.

Eccentric was the operative word.

He was a very tall man, so tall he had to duck to fit through door frames, and his manner of dressing was very unusual. He had on a corduroy suit in a dazzling shade of amethyst purple, black suede shoes, clear round glasses, and an abundance of gothic silver jewelry.

He carried a black cane with a silver tip, and had an explosion of salt and pepper curly hair, except for the bald dome on the top of his head.

He greeted them at the door. "Susie and DeeDee, welcome," he said exuberantly as if they were old friends he hadn't seen in years. "Now, since I'm not endowed with psychic powers, you'll have to let me know which one is which."

DeeDee laughed kindly. "I'm DeeDee, and this is Susie."

"The Deelish caterers," he said. "A play on your name, I presume."

"Yes," DeeDee said. "And you're Tobias Crank, the eminent director, yes?"

"Eminent is a word I cannot claim for myself," he said. "Along with fabulous, multitalented, the Grand Maharaja of Opera, Emperor of the Stage, and other such titles, epithets and descriptions." He winked. "But other people are more than welcome to use them."

He clapped his hands. "Now let us go into the living room briefly, and then into the kitchen."

They walked through a long hallway, decorated with incredible artwork, and into the living room. It was a very large room with a high ceiling and filled with antiques from all over the world.

"You have a fabulous home, Mr. Crank," DeeDee said.

"Oh, I don't own it. I'm just renting it," he said. "Courtesy of a generous benefactor, who sees to it that I have only the grandest and most inspirational nest from where I can rear my baby visions into fully fledged and flying realities."

As they walked farther into the room, a very glamorous African American woman came into view. She was lying on a golden chaise longue, reading a script, her white lacy dress dwarfing her slight frame and skimming the plush carpet beneath her.

Then DeeDee realized who she was – Angel Bridges, the movie star.

Angel looked up, nodded shyly, then went back to her script.

"We'd better not interrupt her," Tobias said in a stage whisper. "She's in 'the zone,' and I don't want to pull her out of it."

When they were in the cavernous kitchen he said, "She's Nefertiti. The best Nefertiti one could ever hope for. She's the epitome of smooth, cool grace, but wonderfully emotive when it's called for. Absolutely superb."

"I expect she also has a great effect on publicity," Susie said. "What with having been in movies and all."

"Yes, indeed," Tobias said, although he sounded and looked less than enthusiastic. "So… the food. I presume you make it elsewhere and bring it here to heat up?"

"Yes, that's correct," DeeDee said. She got a notepad and pen out of her bag. "How many guests are you expecting?"

"Well, it's to be an intimate affair of cast members and prominent opening night guests," he said. "So perhaps thirty."

DeeDee wrote down the number. "Brilliant. And what kind of food were you thinking of serving?"

"You tell me," he said. "You're the experts."

"Well, champagne seems to be in order," DeeDee said, "given that you're celebrating opening night. So perhaps a champagne and hors d'oeuvre reception."

"Naturally," he said.

"Followed by a sit-down dinner," Susie said. "Perhaps six courses?"

"That would be soup, fish, the main course, then cheese, dessert, and coffee," DeeDee said. "Sometimes we do seven, with an amuse-bouche to start, you know, a special little appetizer, but since we're already having hors d'oeuvre, I think that might be overkill."

"Hmm," Tobias said, opening the refrigerator and looking in it. "Overkill is fine, if you'd like. Either way. You know best." He closed the refrigerator and opened the freezer, taking out a medium sized tub of ice cream. "Would you like some?" he asked. "I have to admit that I'm something of an ice cream fiend, so we have pistachio, dulce de leche, chocolate, and a very good vanilla."

"Thank you, but no," DeeDee said politely. "I ate a large breakfast." It was just past nine in the morning, and ice cream seemed like a strange thing to want, since it was November and very cold outside.

"A tub of ice cream is my definition of a good breakfast," Tobias said. He picked up a spoon and dug into the tub of chocolate. "Will you join me, Susie?"

"As a matter of fact, I will," Susie said with a grin. "I'm glad I skipped breakfast this morning."

Tobias smiled. "Oh, a fellow ice cream companion. Goody!" He scooped ice cream out of the tub into a bowl and handed her a spoon.

DeeDee was having a hard time dealing with how bizarre this was all becoming. "So, we'll go with the six courses?"

"Yes," Tobias said firmly. "And I must tell you I can't abide oysters, but I'll eat absolutely anything else. And make it interesting. I want the food to be outstanding."

"Tobias!" came a shout from the other room. It sounded like

Angel.

"Just a moment, ladies," he said, hurrying out of the room with his ice cream tub. He hadn't bothered to put his into a bowl.

DeeDee looked at Susie and raised her eyebrows.

"What?" Susie said, eating her ice cream.

DeeDee grinned. "He's… something."

"I like him," Susie said. "Anyone who's got me eating ice cream at" – she looked at her watch – "9:17 in the morning is good in my book."

DeeDee chuckled. "Yeah. I guess we all have our criteria."

"And don't tell me you didn't expect some theatrical flair from these people. They're artists by profession and artists by nature."

"I guess you're right," DeeDee said. "It should be a fun party if they're all as eccentric as he is."

Susie grinned. "I'll bet."

DeeDee looked down at her notebook. "What do you think we should serve? I like the idea of starting with a beef consommé, but that's hardly earthshattering, is it?"

"No," Susie said. "That would be positively pedestrian for him. We need to think outside the box for this party."

"I agree," DeeDee said. "Let's give ourselves a few days to come up with some ideas and do some research."

Susie nodded. "Sounds good to me."

*****

DeeDee spent the rest of the day doing errands. There were a lot of things to take care of since they'd moved back to the Seattle area, and Jake had been so caught up in his new investigation case he hadn't had time to do much, so the brunt of it fell to her to take care of.

They'd kept her home on Bainbridge Island overlooking Puget Sound. They'd rented it out while they'd been in Connecticut, so thankfully it was more a matter of reacclimating themselves than having to look for somewhere to live. They did have to get some things out of a storage unit they'd rented, such as personal things and one or two valuable antiques they didn't feel comfortable leaving while their house was rented out.

They also had to change back the names on the accounts for their electricity, water, phone line, cable, and internet. There were a lot of other little day-to-day things that they hadn't realized would have to be done, so the "to-do" list ended up being quite long.

Thankfully, Jake and Al had been at home discussing their cases all afternoon, and Al offered to cook dinner. Al didn't cook that often, but when he did, it was really something spectacular. He'd learned all of his uncle's Italian classics – and his uncle had owned one of the most respected restaurants in Naples.

That night was no different. When DeeDee returned home, she found the house smelling absolutely delicious.

The kitchen table was covered with papers, some printed out, some scribbled on with either Jake or Al's equally untidy handwriting, and there was a wonderful surprise sitting on one of the stools at the breakfast bar, sipping a glass of red wine.

"Cassie!" DeeDee said. It was the first time she'd seen her since they'd returned to Seattle.

Cassie jumped up, rushed over to her, and gave her a kiss on the cheek, then a hug. "DeeDee! It's so great to see you."

"Likewise, Cassie. I'm so glad to be back."

They had another quick hug, while Jake and Al looked on, smiling. DeeDee and Jake's husky dogs, Yukon and Balto, were lying in their favorite spot, on the rug in the hallway, a big sleepy lump of overlapping paws. The scene was quite idyllic.

DeeDee went over to Jake, and he hugged her. She didn't approach Al, as he was totally engrossed in his cooking. "It looks and smells like your husband is cooking up a storm, Cassie."

"I try," Al said. "Glad to have you back, DeeDee. And Jake, my partner in crime."

"I don't think you should use that expression, given your history," Jake said with a laugh, pouring and then handing DeeDee a glass of wine.

"Ah, but here's what you don't know. I am secretly still with the mob and here for intelligence purposes," Al said. "I am what they call a mole."

"I'd say more like a rat," Cassie interjected, rolling her eyes.

"Oh, Al, that's wonderful!" DeeDee said. "I'm sure you'll be a lot of use to them. You can begin by telling the mob I'm cooking a six-course dinner for a famous opera director. I'm sure they'll be fascinated by that information."

Al chuckled.

"A six-course dinner?" Jake asked, incredulously. "That's a lot."

"Don't be a philistine, Jake," Cassie said, pouring her wine. "It's not all that unusual."

"I don't even know what that word means, Cassie," Jake said, laughing. "I'm from a humble background where the most courses you got was two, and that was only if you managed to eat all your carrots."

"As a matter of fact, Jake, just for future reference, philistine means someone who has no understanding of culture or the arts."

"Well, I guess I've been put in my place," Jake said with a grin.

"Take no notice of him, Cassie," DeeDee said, waving at Jake with her hand. "I'd love to brainstorm, though. The client says he wants the food to be a conversation starter. If you have any ideas, I'd love to hear them."

"Of course," Cassie said. "I'd be happy to."

"I wanted to hear about your investigation, too." DeeDee said to Jake and Al. "But my brain's too tired for it now. All I want to do is drink more wine, talk to Cassie about menu ideas, and eat what looks like a delicious meal. So, Al, what are you making?"

"A good chef never reveals his secrets."

"Come on, Al, we're going to be eating it in just a few minutes," DeeDee said.

"Exactly!" Al said. "You'll find out then."

It turned out to be a wonderful meal of shrimp stuffed pasta shells, an Italian tomato salad, and for dessert, a fantastic olive oil cake, the recipe of which had come from Al's mother, rather than his uncle. They drank wine, probably a little too much wine, and enjoyed the meal immensely.

Cassie came up with some great ideas for recipes, and Jake and Al spoke late into the night about ideas for the case their firm was handling. By the time Jake and DeeDee fell into bed that night, they were full and happy, warmed by both food and friendship.

CHAPTER TWO

Laurence Powers was extremely drunk. He was sitting on a barstool in a bar several blocks from the hotel in Seattle where he was staying.

He'd been an underage social drinker when he was in high school, but when he began acting at Cambridge University in the Footlights Dramatic Club, he'd taken to drinking with a little more dedication.

He'd suffered from extreme nervous tension as a novice actor, and always had a shot of booze before he went on stage to take the edge off. That had turned into two, three, or four shots, and even though he'd continued to garner wonderful reviews throughout his career, both in Shakespearean plays and operas, which he'd trained for later, he hadn't been able to prevent his long-time habit from slipping out of control.

Why should he? He was above social convention. He was not a simple alcoholic, he told himself. No. He was an actor of the highest caliber and reputation (which was true), who was too lofty to be affected by the drinking (which was untrue). It didn't matter that the rest of his life was in tatters. When he was on the stage, he owned it. The stage was the only important thing in his life. Everything else was irrelevant.

His view hadn't changed in all the years since his lowly start at Cambridge.

And now, in Seattle, opening as the title character in Tobias Crank's *Akhnaten*, he felt vindicated. His career was going swimmingly, thank you very much.

There was just one fly in the ointment.

And, since he'd downed so much whiskey it now leaked out of his pores, he felt uninhibited and free enough to sound off about this to the person nearest to him, in this case, a total stranger.

It happened to be the man in a suit sitting nearby him, not that it would have mattered to Laurence who it was. He just needed a sounding board. He was still sober enough to look the man up and down and scope him out. The man wore a watch, but not a Rolex, and a nice suit, but not Savile Row. More than likely he was successful, but not someone at the very top of the money chain.

"My man," Laurence said, slightly wobbling. "Let me ask you a question?"

The man looked mildly annoyed. "Go ahead."

"Have you ever had someone who was vastly inferior to you steal the limelight from you?" he asked. "In a work situation?"

The man didn't reply, just paid for his drink, got up, and left.

"Hey! I'm talking to you!" Laurence shouted after him, his plummy British accent, the accent of the English upper social class, carrying across the bar. "I'm talking to you!"

But the man walked out without looking back.

"Fine!" Laurence shouted after him. "I rather doubt that you know who I am. I am Laurence Powers, one of the finest Shakespearean actors of this generation!" He swigged back his glass of whiskey. "If not the finest!" He leaned back on the bar with both elbows and looked the bartender dead in the eye. "Give me another one."

The bartender looked doubtful. "Sir, we generally refuse service to…"

"I SAID, GIVE ME ANOTHER ONE!" Laurence bellowed, spit flying onto the bartender's shirt.

"All right," the bartender said in a measured tone. "But this will be your last one."

Laurence leaned back on the barstool and crossed his legs. "Thank you," he said delicately, as if he had been a charming, genteel English gentleman the entire time.

Once the bartender served him another whiskey, Laurence tried to initiate the conversation that was on his mind.

"So sorry, but I didn't catch your name," Laurence said.

"It's Oliver," the bartender said. "Did you say you were a famous Shakespearean actor?"

Laurence was derailed from his intended track of conversation, but it was a welcome derailment. Talking about his fame was one of his favorite pastimes. "Indeed, I am," he said. "A principal player with the Royal Shakespeare Company for a decade."

"Wow," Oliver said, starting to clean some glasses with the spray tap on the sink hose. "That's pretty cool. Is that why you're in town?"

"No," Laurence replied. "I reached the pinnacle there, dominating the Shakespearean world, and I needed a new challenge. I retrained in opera and the rest is history. I'm playing the title role in *Akhenaten* at the Seattle Opera House."

"Nice," Oliver said. "I'm an actor." He nodded at the liquor bottles behind him. "Between jobs."

"Ah, my young man," Laurence slurred. "A kindred spirit, taking your first tentative steps on the glorious road of the stage."

"Well, the screen really," Oliver said. "I was down in Hollywood for a while, auditioning, but nothing really panned out. Got a couple of commercials here and there, but I want a movie role."

"Movies," Laurence sneered. "Yes, they make you a lot of money, and put your face in the papers, but for the discerning person of the arts, the stage is ten times more powerful. Reconsider your career path, my boy. Treading the boards. Hearing the applause, taking the bow, there's no drug like it."

He looked down at his glass. "Except perhaps a nice glass of smooth Macallan scotch." He laughed shakily. "What's your tipple? Allow me…"

"I'm not allowed to drink on the job," Oliver said. "Thanks for the offer, though."

"Not allowed?" Laurence said. "Utter nonsense. You're not a bartender, Orlando, you're an actor."

Oliver didn't bother to correct him. "Maybe another time."

"Yes, fine," Laurence said. "Now, let me give you a few lessons about the acting world. You can thank me later. Some people think that being a movie actor makes them above the rest of the world, and particularly us lowly stage actors. But they have no class. They remind me of the nouveau riche, while we who perform on the stage are the true aristocrats.

"We do it for more than the money. We do it for the love of great art. Then they, with their flashy selves, come along and expect us to bow to the stars of the screen. Well, we shall not! We shall stand, our heads held high, knowing that we are the proud bearers of the torch of culture." He was quite impressed by his own speech, and looked around to see if anyone besides Oliver was listening.

"Don't you think, though, that movies are just modernizing the arts?" Oliver ventured bravely.

Laurence slapped his hands firmly on the bar and wobbled to his right, nearly falling off his barstool. "No, no, not at all! They are cheapening them for the masses to digest. Go to a movie theater and see what movie is playing. Does it move one to tears? Does it reflect deeply on the human condition?"

"Sometimes."

"Rarely!" Laurence countered. "Once in a blue moon. More like sentimental tear-jerkers and armchair psychological analyses. That's what most of these feted screen dramas are. They can never compare to the stage."

"I hear what you're saying," Oliver said. "But there are some great movies out there."

"For instance…?"

"The Shawshank Redemption."

Laurence sipped his whiskey. "I've never heard of it."

"You must have!" Oliver said passionately. He was about to continue, but some other customers were waiting at the bar for drinks. "One moment."

Laurence was too passionate about the subject and too drunk to leave the conversation there, so he continued it on his own. "No, no," he said to himself. "The best films ever made are no match to the pinnacle of the theater. Even half-rate plays outclass them. We are the chosen ones, breathing beauty and art into this dark world." He concluded as he again nearly fell off his barstool.

His phone started to vibrate, but it took him a while to connect the vibration to his phone. He sat, sipping his drink, wondering why his jacket was vibrating.

"Oh!" he said when he realized what he'd been feeling was his phone, and he scrambled to answer it. "Laurence Powers, celebrated Shakespearean actor," he answered in a slur.

"Laurence!" a sharp woman's voice said on the other end of the phone.

"That's me. With whom am I speaking?"

"Your wife, you idiot," the voice said furiously. "You're drunk."

"Not half as drunk as I intend to get, my dear. Why don't you visit me in my hotel?"

"You know perfectly well I'm in London," she said. "Or are you too drunk to remember that? Laurence, you promised me you wouldn't drink while you were over there. You said you'd find an Alcoholics Anonymous meeting to go to, and…"

"You and the bloody AA!" Laurence said, starting to feel a little more alert and sober. He managed to get up off the barstool and walk unsteadily towards the door. He did, however, forget to pay for his drinks. "It is unbecoming of an actor of my stature to go and fraternize with alcoholics."

"Alcoholics like you!" his wife shot back.

"How dare you!"

"And when you're drunk, you do all kinds of stupid things," she said. "Every time you've been unfaithful, it's with a boatload of alcohol in your system. It's only a matter of time before you damage your career by doing something stupid."

"Damage my career?" he said in an incredulous voice. The cold air as he stepped outside the bar was further sobering him up. He walked through the streets as he talked, too incensed to go back to his hotel just yet. "My career is the precious diamond in the center of my heart. I'd do nothing to jeopardize it."

"Don't use that poetic nonsense on me," his wife said.

"If you cut me, I'd bleed the theater."

"Time to grow up, Laurence!" she yelled. "You need to realize we're not all living in the acting fairy tale world you live in. Just do your job over there. Thanks to you squandering money on drink and mistresses and whatever else, we have absolutely no money for retirement. This opera is our retirement money. Don't ruin it or it's all over, Laurence."

"Fine by me," he said, ending the call.

In fact, he was getting sick of her. Camilla Powers. She came from an aristocratic family in England, and they'd met at Cambridge where she was studying medicine. She was now a general practitioner doctor, and he couldn't imagine a more drab, dull, unglamorous, and disgusting profession.

At first, they'd been charmed by each other. She was so different from his first wife. Camilla had been the earth to his air. He was dreamy. She was practical. She helped him get jobs and strategize a plan for his career. He helped her escape the mundane world with his romantic, ethereal ways.

But, far too quickly, in his eyes she'd become a magic-killer who only talked about bills and practicalities. When the veil had lifted from her eyes, Camilla came to see him as an irresponsible drunk who couldn't handle responsibilities and wanted to live as a perpetual idealistic teenager.

The term "Peter Pan Syndrome" often came to her mind when she was thinking of him, someone with an inability to grow up or engage in behavior usually associated with adulthood.

Laurence was so impractical he hadn't even gotten around to divorcing her. He didn't feel he needed to because his heart was in his work and in 'the arts.' She was just the backdrop, albeit a convenient one, since she organized all his affairs.

She was more dissatisfied, but since he was rarely home, it wasn't too much of a toll on her to be married to him. Besides, she wanted her investment of time and effort in him to pay off. She didn't want to be bothered with the rigmarole of divorce or finding someone new, so she didn't initiate a break up.

She called him two more times, because she was stubborn as an ox and clearly wanted to make her point, but so was he. He turned his phone off after the second call and put it back in his jacket. She'd made him absolutely furious, and he started to recall all of their past arguments and the numerous ways he felt she belittled him and his life's work.

As soon as he was on that tangent, his mind went to the current thorn in his side, Angel Bridges, and as he returned to the hotel, he got his phone out and called the director, without really thinking about what he was doing.

"Laurence? Is that you? What on earth is wrong? Why are you calling me at this hour?"

"Angel bleeding Bridges!"

"What about her?" Tobias asked in a panic. "Is she hurt?"

"I wish she was," Laurence said. "I cannot go on like this, Crank. I know you said you couldn't get rid of her for many, many reasons." He rolled his eyes. "Specifically, because people were coming from far and wide to see her. Then you said you couldn't get out of the contract without incurring huge fees that would cripple the production. Then you said... well, who cares what you said? The fact is I refuse to work with her anymore. Your production is not my responsibility."

"Laurence," Tobias said soothingly. "I'm going to work it out. I promise."

"That's what you said before, and yet she's still there, swanning about in her fancy dresses, ignoring your direction, antagonizing me, and generally acting like the Empress of the Universe! I can't take it anymore." The elevator pinged when it got to his floor, and he strode along the corridor, powered by fury.

"I know, Laurence, I know," Tobias said soothingly. "But the two reasons you mentioned still stand. She does draw huge crowds, and I am locked into the contract until the end of the year. If the opera does well, we'll run for a second season, and I won't hire her again, how's that?"

"Not good enough!" Laurence spat. "I'm not quitting, but I'll be damned if that princess dictates where and how I work or don't work. You'd better fix this, Tobias, or I promise, I'll make your life a living hell."

"Are you threatening me, Laurence?"

"You bet I am!"

CHAPTER THREE

It was November again, the month that Siobhan Whitehead most dreaded. And today was the day of the month in November she most dreaded.

She got up and went to the palatial bathroom in the apartment she'd rented while playing Queen Tiye, the mother of Akhnaten, in the production at the Seattle Opera House. She'd been offered a hotel suite, but she preferred to cook her own meals. Having just turned sixty, she had to watch her weight very closely these days, and she didn't want to be tempted by restaurant food.

Except for today.

She looked at herself in the bathroom mirror, makeup free, without her hair done. Raw and real. Tears rolled down her cheeks, because she looked so much like Marina. Or rather, Marina had looked so much like her. Everyone had commented on it. "She's your double." "Did you clone yourself, Siobhan?"

And now she was gone, in the most unexpected of ways.

Siobhan had awakened late, and since she was meeting her ex-husband Walter for an early lunch, she knew she had to start getting ready. After showering, she carefully applied some light makeup. Then she put on a blue dress that Marina had always said she'd loved on her. She did her hair, then set off to meet Walter.

When she arrived at the Indian restaurant, Indian food having been Marina's favorite cuisine, she saw Walter through the window, staring off into space. She watched him for a moment, taking in the deep sadness that was spread across his face. Then he noticed her, waved, and gave her a heartbreaking smile.

She went inside and took off her fur coat. "Someone's waiting for me," she said to the host, without making eye contact.

"Yes, ma'am," he said, taking her coat from her.

Siobhan went over to Walter's table and sat down without a word. They looked at each other for a very long moment. He reached out, took her hand, and squeezed it gently. She squeezed back, then as tears filled her eyes, she pulled her hand away quickly. It had been seven years, and it wasn't getting any easier. If anything, this date that rolled around every year was getting harder and harder to bear.

Still without speaking, Walter poured her a glass of white wine from the bottle he'd ordered. They held their glasses up, and clinked them together.

"To Marina," he said.

"To Marina," she replied hollowly.

They sipped the wine in silence, then Siobhan finally broke it.

"I thought this day would be easier for me to get through as time went on," she said. "But it doesn't. It really doesn't."

"No," he said, looking down at the table. He never had been a man of many words.

"The rest of the year gets easier," she said. "I'm functioning. I'm not sobbing my heart out every day anymore. But when this month comes around it all comes flooding back like it happened yesterday."

"You're keeping busy with the opera," he said. "That's good."

"Are you going to see it while you're in town?" she asked. He had only come to Seattle for their Marina meeting.

"Of course," he said quietly. "If you don't mind, that is."

"I don't mind," she said. "I'd love for you to come, Walter."

He nodded, then looked down again. "Siobhan?" he said.

"Yes."

"Are you sure we did the right thing?"

"Don't bring this back up again," she said, feeling her guts twist inside her. "We tried our best. We took her to that clinic, we tried everything, and I can't bear…"

"No, not that."

"Then what?"

He took a long pause, then said, "Us."

"What about us?"

"Getting divorced," he said. "It would have upset Marina so. She would have wanted us to take comfort in each other, not for her… death… to have driven us apart."

Siobhan felt angry because feeling angry was easier than feeling devastated. "That's what we're doing now, aren't we? Comforting each other?"

"For one day a year."

"You don't remember the year after she died? How we destroyed each other?"

The waiter approached their table to take their orders. They both ordered Marina's favorite, chicken korma and naan bread. Siobhan tried to change the subject.

"Where will we go for the dessert?" she said. "It seems wrong not to eat apple pie, and we're not going to get any here."

"We destroyed each other because we were both deep in grief, Siobhan," Walter said. "We didn't know how to relate to each other. But now…"

"Now we've moved on," she said firmly.

He looked up from his wine glass. "Have you?"

"I don't have another man in my life, if that's what you mean." She took a sip of her wine. "I'm not sure I'll ever have one again. I'm too tired."

"I haven't been with anyone since you, either."

"That doesn't mean we should be together."

"But don't you think…"

"Look, Walter, today is supposed to be about Marina. Not about you and me."

He leaned back. "Yes, you're right."

"You know I'm donating to the charity that provides support for families affected by heroin use," she said. "I'm organizing a fundraiser with them for when I get back to New York. Would you like to be involved?"

"Of course," he said. "What kind of fundraiser?"

"A silent auction. The opera set, and some art dealers. I'm hoping it will raise a lot of money. If it's a success, it will allow them to provide more support to the families.”

“That’s wonderful.” He sighed. “If only there was a foolproof way to treat the addiction. Like a pill. You just take it, and then boom, you’re back to the way you were before.”

Siobhan smiled sadly. “It would be wonderful.”

“It all seems so terminal,” he said. “Supporting families affected. Like the person taking the heroin is beyond help.”

Siobhan pushed back tears that threatened to trickle from her eyes. “They do offer treatment. But… sometimes, it seems they are beyond help. But there are some success stories…” Her eyes welled up, her throat choked up, and she couldn’t speak anymore.

Walter leaned over and rubbed her arm.

“Don’t,” she said, pushing him away gently. “I’ll start sobbing. Let’s talk about happier times.”

Walter nodded. “That’s a good idea. I brought the album with me. Maybe after lunch we can find a place for apple pie and look over the pictures.”

“Yes,” Siobhan said. “Not now.” She didn’t want to cry. “So, let’s start from the beginning. That positive pregnancy test, after all those years of trying.”

“One of the best days of my life,” Walter said.

“What were the others?”

“Her being born. And marrying you.”

They didn’t need to talk about the worst days – they knew them very well.

Their kormas soon arrived and they spoke about Marina in great detail. Her birth, which was surprisingly smooth and uneventful. How Siobhan had cried out, "My little girl! My girl!" when she was born. Her first words, first steps. How she'd been so full of smiles and laughter as a baby.

Then, her first days in preschool, then in a bigger school. How she'd always put on plays for them, dancing and singing around the living room, and acting out a million different characters.

"Acting is in the blood," they'd said at the time, and they said it again now.

They managed to lose themselves in memories of her childhood and began to smile. The Christmas she'd given them handmade bags she'd sewed by hand at school, with wobbly 'Mummy' embroidered onto one, and wobbly 'Daddy' onto the other. Siobhan had said she still had hers.

"I have mine, too," Walter had said.

They spoke about how she'd begged for a little brother, but they weren't able to have any more children. Doctors had told them Marina was the only little miracle they were going to get. Marina was lavished with all the attention and affection they had. She was the center of their world.

At the time, Siobhan had only taken opera jobs in New York and had turned down several spectacular career opportunities. She wanted to be with Marina, because she was more important than her career. Walter ran his own accounting firm and changed his hours so he could be home with Marina when she came home from school, the days Siobhan worked. Neither of them wanted to get a nanny.

As Marina grew up, it appeared her love for singing, dancing, and acting was not just child's play. It was a real passion. She joined a local performing arts group, nothing prestigious, just a regular after-school and Saturday club. Siobhan had always wanted Marina to do whatever the little girl's heart desired and refused to be a pushy stage parent. Once or twice, she even tried to discourage Marina from showbusiness, but Marina was not to be dissuaded. She wanted to light up the stage and screen.

She went to a full-time acting school when she was sixteen and quickly got a few jobs. Nothing earth shattering, but beginner's jobs that would look good on her resume. She had a boyfriend and everything looked great.

One day she'd come into the kitchen squealing with excitement. "Mom, I've got this. I've got this. I've got this. I have to get this! There's an audition coming up for the lead in a movie in Hollywood, and they've called me to read for it."

The whole family was excited.

But Marina didn't get the job.

"Don't worry, honey," Siobhan had said, stroking her hair. "This is showbiz. You'll get another audition soon. A better one."

But something had changed in Marina. She didn't go to auditions anymore. After that it was a very quick descent into partying, alcohol, party drugs, and finally heroin.

All Siobhan's belief systems crashed. She'd thought a little girl so loved could never be swallowed up by the monster that was heroin. But she'd been wrong.

CHAPTER FOUR

Lola Newman was on her way to give an interview to an arts and culture magazine. They'd wanted to get Angel Bridges, but Angel turned down interviews with such lowly publications. It was likely she was doing interviews with TIME and all the glossy women's magazines with circulations of hundreds of thousands.

Lola was bitterly thinking about all of this as she made her way to the Seattle Opera House in a cab. She stepped out into the bracing wind and walked up the steps. Her hair flew everywhere in the icy breeze, and even though she was a little late, she rushed to the restroom before meeting the reporter in the lobby.

Once she was in there, she took out a brush and smoothed her hair down. She also reapplied her red lipstick. They weren't going to take her picture, since they'd told her they were going to use the publicity photos, but she still wanted to look her best.

She always did, and loved the looks and double takes she got wherever she went. The only thing was, she wished they were looking at her because they knew who she was, like they did with Angel Bridges. But she was still an unknown. Just an understudy, or what they called a cover in the opera world, but not the star.

Lola knew she couldn't show the world her bitterness. She was smart enough to know she had to hide it and be charming and nice.

She'd mastered it to a tee.

She walked out of the restroom into the lobby, blonde hair swishing, heels click-clacking on the tile floor, flashing a big red lipstick smile. Lola was ready to be presented to the world.

"Ms. Newman?" a woman said, coming toward her.

"That's me."

"I'm Erica from the magazine. Shall we sit down and have coffee?"

"Sure!" Lola said, shaking the woman's hand. "Lovely to meet you, Erica."

They sat down, drank their coffee, and Lola's mask of a smile never faded. Erica adjusted her phone so she could record their meeting.

"So…" Erica said. "Tell me. Who are you dating right now?"

Lola rolled her eyes internally. It was clear Erica wanted gossip. She wanted an edgy article. Something tantalizing. Lola could see why, because the magazine she worked for was deathly boring. Maybe they wanted to expand their readership and get a juicy quote to splash all over the front cover.

But then, Lola thought, *this could work to my advantage.*

"I'm not going to say my needs aren't being fulfilled," Lola said, giving Erica a knowing look, "but I'm always open to new offers."

"Ah," Erica said, unable to keep a smile from her face. "And what is it you look for in a man?"

"I'm not going to lie, I like an older man, but that's usually because they have a certain gravitas, a confidence that comes with age. I'm open to younger men, too, that have the same trait." She giggled. "I guess I just find confidence irresistible."

Erica nodded, grinning. "Well, you don't seem short on confidence yourself, so I suppose you need a man to match you. That said, are there any insecurities buried under the surface?"

A boatload, Lola thought.

"I don't think so," Lola said. "I believe I just got lucky when God was giving out confidence. Besides, if you're going to be in the performing arts, it's no good being a wallflower."

"You say that," Erica said, "but I've known a number of actors who were quite shy in real life. Apparently when you're playing so many different characters and getting so deeply immersed in being them, it's easy to lose yourself."

Lola laughed in a charming way. "You're quite the psychologist, Erica," she said. "I just don't think that way. I have a very strong sense of self."

"Hmm," Erica said, seemingly disappointed. "Other phenomena I've noticed in actors include substance abuse and unstable relationships."

Lola's mouth twitched, giving away her annoyance. "You don't seem to like actors much, do you? Anyway, I consider myself to primarily be a singer. The acting is secondary in the opera."

"Yes, I know you studied at the Vanderbilt University Blair School of Music."

"You've done your research," Lola said. "I enjoyed it immensely. It's made me the woman I am today."

"Describe that woman," Erica said.

"Okay… a young, ambitious woman, ready for the next step in her career."

"Aha," Erica said, eyes shining. "You must be devastated not to have been cast as Nefertiti, but instead, as the cover for Angel Bridges."

"Not at all," Lola said. "Angel Bridges deserved the part. I'm honored to be her cover. I'm sure I'll get my turn in the future to be cast in a leading role."

"That's a very diplomatic answer," Erica said. "The perfect answer. The professional answer. What about the personal answer? The heart of hearts answer?"

"Haha, well, that would be telling."

"You can tell me," Erica said. "I won't judge you. Many people in your position would be very frustrated."

"I'm covering the lead role in *Akhnaten* under a celebrated director, in the Seattle Opera House. I'm perfectly happy with that." She wasn't of course, but Erica's insinuations were hurting her pride, and she didn't want to admit it.

"You're happy with that," Erica said. "Fair enough. It's just you mentioned you are ambitious. And I know ambitious people like to compare themselves with others. Their schoolmates, in particular. Your schoolmate, Zara Roland, is playing Minnie in *La fanciulla del West* in the Sydney Opera House." She looked up at Lola and smiled. "That's got to sting a little, right?"

"I wish her all the best," Lola said as she flashed a smile. Of course it stung. She'd obsessed for weeks over it, telling everyone how she'd always outranked Zara by miles in all their classes. Plus, Lola was much prettier. How had Zara been cast in such an amazing role? It wasn't fair at all.

Erica sighed. "All right. So tell me, Lola, is it true, as people say, that Angel Bridges is a total diva who won't follow direction and does as she pleases? How do the two of you get along? It doesn't sound like she creates an easy working atmosphere."

Now Lola really had to grit her teeth. Angel Bridges had never been rude to her. That would have been quite easy to deal with. Lola could have been rude back, and gossiped about her in private, and maybe even publicly tarnished Angel's name, as long as she could have made herself out to be a victim.

No, Angel hadn't been rude to her at all. What she'd done was much more humiliating. She hadn't paid Lola any attention at all. Angel didn't argue with anyone except Laurence, who seemed to trigger something in her. She didn't even argue with Tobias when she disagreed with his directing. She just nodded, and quietly went ahead and did her own thing. She never engaged with Lola beyond a nod.

When Lola had complained to Tobias about it, he'd told her that Angel Bridges, with her vast experience and fame, had earned the right to ignore her. He was sympathetic, in a way, but it had only enraged Lola even more.

Lola desperately wanted to vent her rage, but her fake smile stayed firmly in place. She knew that badmouthing a star like Angel Bridges would be a bad career move. She didn't want to be painted as difficult to work with.

Lola hid all her fury inside and said sweetly, "She's very professional, and I feel honored to work with such a versatile and experienced actor such as Angel."

"Some people would feel like their personal territory had been taken over. After all, she's a movie actress, not someone renowned for opera. Most of the world didn't even know she could sing. It was a sensation. All that attention that's been paid to her must make some opera players such as yourself feel a little jealous."

"You seem to talk about jealousy a lot," Lola said, her smile never wavering. "I'm not really the jealous type."

"Oh, really?" Erica said, a gleeful grin lighting up her face. "That's not what I heard from your previous colleagues in Maine, who told me you were devastated not to have been cast as Pamina but rather

Papagena, and told everyone who would listen that you were planning to break Georgina Hofer's legs. She was the actress who got the part of Pamina."

Lola's heart began to race. "Oh dear. It seems people have dreadfully active imaginations. I was delighted to get the role of Papagena, and I received excellent reviews. I merely told Georgina to 'break a leg.' It's a show business expression. I'm sure you've heard of it."

Erica narrowed her eyes. "Don't opera singers usually say *in bocca al lupo*? You know, good luck in Italian. It's my understanding that those are the words that are used in the opera genre."

"Well, yes, but break a leg is perfectly acceptable, too."

Erica raised her eyebrows and looked down at her notes. She shuffled through some papers, clearly trying to think of something that would make a juicy story.

"Is that all?" Lola said sweetly. "I really have to be going." She picked up her purse and stood up.

"Fine," Erica said, thunder passing over her face. "Perhaps another time. Maybe I'll catch you after opening night."

"That would be lovely. Wonderful to meet you." Lola walked away, out of the opera house, and her expression turned just as sour as Erica's. The woman had really gotten under her skin.

CHAPTER FIVE

The day of the opera's opening night soon rolled around, and Susie and DeeDee were at DeeDee's house that morning, putting the finishing touches on the food items they'd been making for the last couple of days.

The menu had been decided and cleared with Tobias Crank a week earlier, and was, in Tobias' own words, "wonderfully eccentric."

The soup course was a peanut butter and lamb soup called Nkatenkwan, a recipe originating in Ghana.

The fish was a spicy crab egg salad from Thailand.

The main course was pork cooked in lime and caramel, over a bed of wild black rice, which was Vietnamese-inspired.

The cheese course was the least adventurous – fried gorgonzola.

Then came the dessert, sweet ravioli stuffed with rum and banana, with a ricotta cheese ice cream.

Needless to say, the preparations needed were no mean feat. Thankfully, they'd prepared a lot of the food over the previous days. The ice cream was in the freezer, as was the ravioli. They would defrost the ravioli cases and assemble them at the last minute, since the banana needed to be fresh.

The gorgonzola was the only other thing that needed to be done when they were at Tobias' apartment, so everything else could be done ahead of time.

DeeDee cooked two huge pans of Nkatenkwan, while Susie prepared the lime and caramel sauce. She'd had to feed Yukon and Balto a large amount of food and send them outside in the backyard to play together, otherwise she knew the kitchen smells would have them gravitating toward the stove, begging for a taste.

"Ugh," DeeDee said, as she came out of the kitchen and onto the porch, her face red from the heat of the kitchen and the stress. "I love cooking, but seriously, why do I do this to myself?"

"Because you're the best," Jake said, not looking up from his papers. He was sitting in the rocking chair on the porch, looking through them.

"How's the case going?" DeeDee asked. "Please take my mind off peanut butter and lamb soup."

Jake looked up at her and sighed. "I'm nervous, DeeDee. I can't lie. This particular case is really big. We're looking into a potential white-collar crime case. Insider trading, doctoring accounts, the whole lot. The company is a mess."

"Isn't that something for the police to look into?"

Jake sighed. "It should be. But the owner of the company, Mark Jessup Sr., is the only one who's gotten wind of it. He's been planning to hand the company over to his two sons, Joshua and Paul, but he thinks one of them is responsible for what's been done. He'd rather find out himself and oust the guilty son, without getting the police involved."

"Because it's his son."

"That, and he doesn't want the reputation of the company tarnished," Jake said. "He thinks they'd lose clients, and I have to say he's probably right."

"What kind of a company is it?"

"Accounting and tax advisors for big corporations," Jake said. "It's huge."

"Right… so why are you nervous?"

"There have been a couple of incidents with some of his staff at the company. One had a car accident and died. Another supposedly shot himself. There's a woman who just disappeared and is now reported as a missing person. But Al and I think these things are all connected to the shady things going on at the company.

"Al's going into the company today, posing as a Mafia guy gone good who has a big construction company and needs advice." He breathed out deeply. "I just hope it goes well. I'm worried about him."

"Al's a convincing actor," DeeDee said. "Remember when we were trying to track down his potential killer in Chicago? He had to do his fair share of acting then, and he certainly pulled it off."

"Yeah," Jake said. "I just hope he can pull it off this time."

DeeDee walked over and put her arms around Jake. "I'd love to stay and talk about it, but I have too much work to do. I'm sure Al will be fine. He can take care of himself. Look at his background. I mean if anyone can protect himself, he can."

"I suppose you're right," Jake said.

"I hope you're not planning to sit at home all day worrying about him," DeeDee said. "You'll drive yourself crazy. Go running or do something. Get your bicycle out of the garage. It must be covered in dust, but it would be good for you to get some exercise."

"You're right," Jake said. "I'll try to do something."

"Just make sure you're here when we're ready to load things into the van," DeeDee said. "That vat of soup is going to be a killer."

DeeDee went back inside to join Susie and to tend her soup.

They weren't due at the apartment until 9:00 p.m., since *Akhnaten* wouldn't be over until 11:00 p.m., so they had plenty of time to kill. After Jake helped them load everything into the van, except the things that needed to be frozen or refrigerated, Susie went home for a nap and a shower, and DeeDee decided to do the same. It was going to be a very late night, with dinner not due to start until midnight.

DeeDee had thought that was a little crazy, but Susie had said, "Hey, that's Tobias Crank for you." As it turned out, there was actually an opening night dinner pre-performance with a ticket price per head of $2,000, starting at 5:30 p.m. But Tobias Crank said a full stomach would mess with his nerves, and he couldn't possibly have his cast eating a heavy dinner before the performance.

"That dinner is for our audience," he'd said. "This dinner is for us, and we plan to party the night away." It was a Saturday night, and their next performance was a Wednesday matinee, so they had plenty of time in between to recover.

When DeeDee woke up from her nap, she found Balto lying next to her, snuggling. She stroked him, and he looked up at her happily. When she got up, he followed at her heels. She also found Jake looking much happier than when she'd gone upstairs. She grinned. "I take it Al's performance went off without a hitch?"

"It did," Jake said. "He doesn't have any info yet, but he's got one of the brothers, Joshua Jessup, on his side. He's working to get close to him and see what intel he can squeeze out of him. He's arranging an expensive dinner at Canlis next weekend to soften him up."

"Canlis? It's only the premier luxury restaurant in the city. Very nice! That's going to be one large item on his expense account."

Jake chuckled. "Got to impress, you know. I told him I was going along, not with him, but at another table, just to keep an eye on things. I was wondering if you wanted to go with me."

"Ahh, how romantic. A stakeout date."

Jake pulled her into a hug. "Sorry. It's not a stakeout, though."

"Will I be expected to wait for you to jump to your feet at any moment, gun in hand, ready to blast the restaurant apart?"

"No!" he said, laughing. "Not at all."

"I'll think about it," DeeDee said. "But on first thought, it doesn't sound very relaxing to me."

"Honestly, I'm just going as a precaution," Jake said. "There's a 99% chance of smooth sailing. No, make that a 99.9% chance."

DeeDee smiled. "Well, all right, then. Cassie's told me it's very good."

"In that case, I'd like to find out with you." He gave her a quick kiss on the lips. "If for no other reason, take pity on me eating my dinner at the top restaurant in Seattle all by myself."

DeeDee smiled and kissed him back. "Oh, fine. Just don't try and use your puppy dog eyes on me."

On cue, he did.

She swiped his arm and said, "I've got to go shower now. It's a big night for me."

"You're going to do awesome," he said. "I just know it."

*****

When it was 8:00 p.m., DeeDee loaded the refrigerated and frozen items into the van and soon she was on her way. She'd kissed Jake and told him she and Susie were staying at Cassie and Al's apartment in Seattle, because they wouldn't be able to make the last ferry of the night to return to Bainbridge Island.

She picked Susie up and Susie drove. DeeDee didn't really like driving the big van, but Susie was in her element. She smiled and hummed a cheerful tune.

DeeDee looked over at her and chuckled. "Why are you so happy?"

"The check we've gotten for this party alone could hold us for three or four months, even if we didn't get any more jobs. We could sit around and do nothing for weeks. Imagine."

"We're not going to do that," DeeDee said. "We're not in it just for the money, Susie!"

"I know," Susie said. "You didn't let me finish. I was going to say, and we've opened ourselves up to a whole new market. Multiple courses of weird and wonderful foods from around the globe for high-end clients who want to show off how cultured and interesting they are. And these kinds of clients always want to pay top dollar. In fact, the more, the better."

DeeDee smiled. "You're right, Susie. And you know something, I've really enjoyed planning the menu and cooking new kinds of food. It's all so interesting."

"It is," Susie responded. "I think if we found ourselves doing another dull corporate dinner right after this one, we might just feel a little bored."

"Well, if it puts money in the bank..." DeeDee said. "But I do understand what you're saying. This is exciting."

"Yes, it is, both from a culinary and business perspective."

"Agreed, and I really hope they like it."

Once the ferry let them off in Seattle, they picked up two of the waiters they'd hired for the event, so they'd have some help with carrying and serving things.

Tobias had given them a set of keys to his apartment, since he refused to have an assistant take care of things for him. "They never get it quite right," he'd said on the phone. They let themselves in and the four of them unloaded everything. They'd brought along a two-wheeled dolly to help them, which made things much easier.

Then they began preparing everything, so that as soon as the hors d'oeuvre were out, they'd pretty much be on cruise control, and it should be easy.

"Looks like we're ready," DeeDee said, flopping against the counter. "But I could really use a nap about now."

"Or a cup of coffee," Susie said, switching on the coffee machine. "DeeDee, this is a very expensive coffee machine. It must have cost thousands of dollars. What would you like?"

"Just a flat white," DeeDee said. "I was thinking maybe a double espresso, but I'd better pace myself. I'll probably have more later on, and the last thing I need is for my hands to be shaking while I'm trying to plate all of these dishes. Thanks, Susie."

"Flat white coming up," Susie said, and made herself a cappuccino. The two waiters had espressos.

DeeDee looked at her watch. "It's 10:00 p.m. now. They'll start arriving in just a little more than an hour from now."

The rest of the waiters, a veritable army, arrived about fifteen minutes later, and Susie briefed them. She'd printed out a number of instruction sheets, since they'd learned that if you only have three or four, invariably they get lost. The kitchen was littered with them. Susie looked around the kitchen with a grin and said, "The more the better."

Soon it was time to start getting the champagne glasses ready and plating the hors d'oeuvre. Before long, DeeDee heard the noises of people talking and shouting joyously. The opening night show had obviously been a triumph.

"They're here!" she said to the wait staff. She grinned, feeling butterflies of nervousness flutter in her stomach. "Here we go!"

CHAPTER SIX

Immediately upon arriving at his apartment after leaving the Seattle Opera House, Tobias Crank came into the kitchen looking positively elated. He used grand gestures with his hands, and his voice was booming. "Well, hello my lovelies! How are we doing?"

Susie was ushering the waiters with the champagne outside, so DeeDee maneuvered Tobias away from the doorway. "We're doing great, thank you. This is really exciting," she said. "I take it opening night was a success?"

"Not just a success. It was a runaway success!" he exclaimed. "After the curtain came down, there was a seventeen-minute standing ovation!"

"Wow," DeeDee said. "That's a very long time."

"Yes," Tobias said gleefully, clapping his hands together. "It was absolutely wonderful. Laurence Powers was particularly outstanding. The audience lapped him up."

"And Angel Bridges?"

"Well, yes, the audience liked her, too," he said, but less enthusiastically. "Now, I came in here to bring you out to meet our benefactor. He's an art dealer from New York. He wanted to meet you because of your most unusual menu."

"Not to scold me, I hope," DeeDee said.

"On the contrary. Do come along," he said as he beckoned to her.

She followed him into another living room, one she'd not seen before. There were a few people milling around with glasses of champagne, looking impossibly glamorous in their evening wear. Tobias led her over to the Chesterfield armchairs and sofas by the fireplace.

Sitting in one of the armchairs was a very imposing man. Although he was quite small and very slight, actually a much smaller man than average, and very elderly, it was his manner and the look in his eyes that made him so striking. He had on an expensive-looking suit, and he had a gray beard. When he stood up DeeDee saw how very short he was. He moved very slowly, yet gracefully. "So this is the creative chef we owe our fabulously interesting menu to," he said.

"Indeed it is," Tobias said. "Lowell, I would like to introduce you to DeeDee Wilson, who is the one responsible for coming up with such an exotic menu of dishes for us to enjoy. DeeDee, this is Lowell Marks, our generous benefactor."

Lowell took her hand and smiled. "I don't know about generous," he said. "Rather selfish, I think. I see my investments in the arts as indulgences, Ms. Wilson."

"Indulgences that benefit a lot of people," DeeDee replied.

"Yes," Tobias said, looking rather nervous, which DeeDee didn't understand. "Please, sit down."

DeeDee sat down opposite Lowell, and he inquired about the menu. He had such an authoritative, calm, quiet air about him that DeeDee felt like she might be speaking to a king. In all honesty, it made her a little uncomfortable.

"I got a seventeen-minute standing ovation, didn't I?" a voice from behind them said loudly. DeeDee turned and saw that the angry comment had come from Angel, who was speaking to Tobias. They were having a very animated conversation as both of them left the room.

That jolted DeeDee back to reality. She looked at her watch. "I'd better get back to the kitchen, Mr. Marks."

"Please, call me Lowell."

"Lowell," she said with a smile. "I need to make sure that everything is under control for dinner."

"Great," Lowell said. "I'm looking forward to it."

DeeDee left the room, and started walking down a hallway towards the kitchen. She heard an aggressive tone of voice coming from someone on the stairwell. As she walked down the hall, she couldn't see who it was and she could only hear the voice. She paused for a moment to listen.

"I was the one who got a seventeen-minute standing ovation," Tobias hissed. "I'm the director. You're only a body and an operatic voice. You're meant to do what I say. They were much more enamored with Laurence than they were with you."

"So you say," Angel angrily retorted.

"You're making my life hell with your refusal to take my direction," Tobias said. "I'll be so glad to see your back as you go out the door at the end of the season."

"Whatever," Angel said. "Just know that it will be at the end of the season, because you signed a contract, and you won't be getting out of it without very expensive consequences."

Realizing she was eavesdropping, DeeDee quickly hurried away. When she got back to the kitchen, she found Susie getting ready to serve the first two courses, the soup and the crab egg salad. She had waiters and waitresses buzzing around her, following her orders.

DeeDee smiled. "Looks like everything is going well. Where can I jump in?"

"Nowhere," Susie said. "I've got everything under control, so don't come in and mess it up. You know the saying about too many cooks spoiling the broth. I've got Tanya here as my right-hand woman, and we're a good team. You can come back in time to take the pork out."

DeeDee laughed and sipped a glass of champagne. "Fine by me."

It turned out to be a good thing, because Tobias Crank seemed to think DeeDee should be introduced to everyone.

She met the conductor, an overweight man with a thatch of blond hair, who was a little bumbling, but overall nice.

Next was Laurence Powers, who was already very drunk and downed an entire glass of champagne during their very brief conversation. He had an upper-class English accent and impeccable manners, but the manners seemed empty, like there was no genuine kindness behind them. He went on and on about his Shakespearean acting career.

She met Angel Bridges again, who was somewhat reserved, but friendly enough.

Then there was Siobhan Whitehead, who was around sixty, a really graceful and gracious woman who asked about DeeDee's catering business and really seemed to be interested in what she had to say.

She also met the character, Horemhab, who was played by a young man called Will. He was a Texan and very friendly. Then there was the man who played the High Priest of Amon who was from Ireland and seemed rather uncomfortable with small talk.

At the agreed upon time, Tobias Crank called everyone to dinner. The waiter and waitress army sprang into action, and the soup went out.

DeeDee and Susie were left alone in the kitchen. "The moment of truth," DeeDee said, biting her lip.

"I know. I hope they like it," Susie replied.

As it turned out, they didn't have to wait too long to find out how the food was going down.

Tanya came back into the kitchen with the other waiters when the soup course had been served, and said, "Tobias asks if you can both come out. He wants to see you."

Susie and DeeDee looked at each other, a little nervously. Would it be good news or bad news? Tanya didn't give anything more away, so they walked out to the dining room to find out. DeeDee rubbed her hands on her pants to get the sweat off of them.

As soon as they came through the door, the room burst into applause.

DeeDee jumped, then put her hand to her mouth. "My goodness."

She looked at Susie, who was laughing.

Tobias stood up, leading the applause, beaming at them. The other guests stood up as well.

My, oh my, DeeDee thought. *I could get used to these operatic people. A standing ovation, just for us.* She didn't really like being the center of attention, but she could see the humor and find the joy in the situation. Susie was positively reveling in it.

The applause continued for a minute or so, then Tobias waved his hand, and it died out as people sat down.

"We brought you out here to show you our appreciation of the magnificent food," he said. "It is most unusual and has sparked a great deal of conversation." He gave them a meaningful look and a raised eyebrow, clearly letting them know they had met his criteria for creative cooking.

"You're most welcome. It's been our pleasure," DeeDee said.

"I shall be sure to pass on your details to everyone in case they may be catering a party," Tobias said. "Or perhaps I'll keep you as my own exclusive secret. What do you say?"

Susie laughed. "We'd be delighted either way. Exotic haute cuisine for a culinary adventure!"

"Indeed!"

"We'd better get back to check on the main course," DeeDee said.

"Please, please, don't let us keep you," Tobias said. "Outstanding work. Outstanding."

As they returned to the kitchen, DeeDee said, "Exotic haute cuisine? Culinary adventure? You didn't make that up on the spot, did you?"

"Well, no," Susie admitted. "I've been thinking this over, like I mentioned earlier. I think we can incorporate this into our business model in a new way. You know, like advertise in luxury magazines. Put our name out there."

"I must admit, I didn't want to get too excited about this, but now that they've been so enthusiastic about the food, it's given me confidence. Maybe we really can do this."

Susie flashed her a smile. "I know we can do this. More fun, more money… what's not to like about that?"

"You missed your calling, Susie. You should be a salesperson,"

DeeDee said with a laugh. "All right, when this is over, let's have a business meeting and talk about the new direction."

"You're on," Susie said as they went back into the kitchen.

The waiters were streaming out of the room with the crab egg salad course.

"Let's get going on this pork," DeeDee said.

"Yes, let's," Susie agreed.

The evening passed smoothly. It was a little stressful getting all the courses out as scheduled, it always was, but there were no major problems, which was a relief. The pork didn't burn, the ice cream didn't melt on the plates before it was served, and there were no other flies in the ointment.

That is, until the very end of the meal. The guests began to leave the dining room and go into the rest of the apartment. Everyone was full and satisfied from the meal, as well as being quite relaxed from copious amounts of wine. Some were talkative, while others were sleepy, especially since it was so late. The performers in particular looked a little droopy. DeeDee stood at the kitchen door and watched them all leave with a small, satisfied, tired smile on her face. It had certainly been a good day.

Until there was a terrible scream, which sent chills down DeeDee's spine.

"She's dead!" someone frantically screamed. "She's dead!"

CHAPTER SEVEN

In less than an hour, the party had turned into a crime scene, complete with a forensic team, several detectives, and a number of officers.

Everyone was instructed to gather in the dining room, including DeeDee, Susie, and the wait staff. They all sat in silence, looking at each other. Tobias Crank was white as a sheet, and looked like he might throw up at any moment.

The body of Angel Bridges, covered in a white sheet, was wheeled on a gurney past the open doorway, and there were several gasps as it went by.

After what seemed like an eternity, the lead detective came into the room. "Hello, everybody. My name is Detective Kirton. We are going to interview everyone, but not at this stage. My officers will be asking you for your contact information, and you will all be called in for an interview over the next couple of days."

Everyone gave their contact details. DeeDee and Susie were not permitted to take back any of their catering equipment. Everything in the apartment had to be left as it was, so they left with an empty van. They gave Tanya a ride back home.

"I can't believe it," Susie said. "It's so surreal."

DeeDee nodded. "I know. Everything was going so well, and then…" Her mind replayed the events of the night. "Hang on," she said. "Tanya, you were in the dining room the whole time. You saw Angel leave the room to take a call, right?"

"Yes," Tanya said. "She looked quite distressed."

"So that must mean you saw the murderer leave the room, too."

"Whoa Deedee, we don't even know if it's a murder," Susie pointed out. "It could have been natural causes."

"It could," DeeDee agreed, "but I've got a gut feeling that she didn't die from natural causes. So my question to you, Tanya, remains the same. Did you see anyone leave?"

"I don't know," Tanya said. "Quite a few people left the table at some point or other. To smoke, I think, or go to the bathroom."

"Can you remember who?" DeeDee said.

Tanya screwed up her face.

"Don't interrogate the poor girl," Susie said.

"Sorry," DeeDee said. "With a private investigator husband, I guess it comes naturally."

"No, it's okay," Tanya said. "I'm just trying to remember. I know Tobias Crank left the room at some point. I remember, because he's so strange-looking, isn't he? He was sitting right in front of where I was standing, and he told the person next to him he was going to the bathroom. Oh, and that one who was always going on about being a famous Shakespearean actor."

"Laurence Powers," DeeDee said.

"I'm not sure of his name. The English one."

"Yes, that's him. So he left the table, too?"

"Yes."

"Anyone else?" DeeDee asked.

"A few ladies went out, older ladies and younger ones, but I can't say I recognized any of them. They could have been big opera stars, and I still wouldn't have known. I'm not much into opera."

"Well, it's good that you know Laurence and Tobias went out," DeeDee said. "That could help the investigation."

"I'm dreading being interviewed." Tanya fiddled with her fingers, pushing her cuticles back. "Police make me nervous."

"I'm not exactly looking forward to it either," Susie said. "I thought this was going to be a wonderful start for us with exotic gourmet catering. Now people will probably think there's a curse on us and refuse to hire us. Given all that's happened before…"

"They won't," DeeDee said. "People can't be that superstitious."

"You'd be surprised," Susie said.

"No," DeeDee said firmly. "Everything will be fine."

They dropped Tanya off at her apartment and DeeDee and Susie went to Cassie and Al's apartment for a well-deserved sleep.

*****

The following morning when she got home, Jake was waiting for her. She'd given him a call the night before to tell him the dinner had gone well and that she'd fill him in on the details when she got home.

He opened the front door for her before she could get her key out. "Are you okay? You don't look too good. Is something wrong?" Yukon and Balto rushed up to her as well. It was like they could sense something had happened.

"Yes, I'm fine," she said, hugging him. "The same can't be said for Angel Bridges, though. She died at the dinner party." She knelt down and hugged Yukon and Balto.

"What?" he said, closing the door behind them. "Really? Do they think it was from natural causes or murder…? Do they know who did it, if it was murder?"

"Well, no one was arrested," DeeDee said. She sighed, stretched and yawned, a look of exhaustion on her face. "I had a hard time sleeping last night, and I'm really tired." She looked over at the table, where his papers were strewn. "Were you up late working on your case?"

"Yes," he said, "But forget that. I want you to tell me what happened while I make you some tea."

"That would be nice," she said as she sat down at the kitchen table. "Well, she was found dead on the balcony. I rushed over to where she was after someone discovered her, but didn't see much."

"Was there blood?"

"No," she said. "So maybe it was natural. She was relatively young, but it could have been a heart attack or something."

"She was a huge star," Jake said. "This is going to be all over the news."

"Yes… I suppose it could have been murder, too. Honestly, my gut feeling is that it was. The police are calling everyone in for an interview over the next couple of days, so I'm sure we'll find out."

"Good grief," Jake said. "If it is murder, do you have a sense of who it could be?"

"Not really," DeeDee said. "One of our waitresses mentioned

some people who left the dining room during the meal. Someone would have had to have left the room to do it. But it's hard to remember things like who left the room when there was no need to pay attention to it at the time."

"Yes," Jake said. "That's true."

"Anyway, I'm sure the police will do their job. Susie and I just need to focus on finding some new clients and putting this whole thing behind us. We decided to go after some more unusual clients, so we can be more experimental with the dishes we prepare for clients. I sure hope this event isn't a bad omen."

"I don't think it will be," Jake said. "I'm sure it was just bad luck, and the two of you will do spectacularly."

"I hope so." Jake brought over the tea, and she took it from him.

"Thank you. Any updates on your investigation? Found anything out?" DeeDee asked.

"Not yet," Jake said. "Just trying to pull out some info that Al can slip into the conversation when he meets up with Joshua Jessup, you know, kind of to gain his trust and wiggle some more information out of him. I'm going to keep combing through this stuff."

"Sounds sensible," she said with a sigh. "Let's talk about something else. Something to look forward to." She stroked Balto on the head and he nuzzled into her knee.

"Shoot."

"I was hoping you'd come up with a topic, but okay. Hmm... When are we going to have our next vacation, and where should we go?"

"Once this case is wrapped up, I could go," Jake said, "providing your catering business will allow it."

"How long do you think that might be?"

"How long is a piece of string?" He grimaced apologetically. "That's one downside about this line of work. The complete unpredictability of it. While I enjoy the thrill of the work, being my own boss, and the pay, it's also hard to just switch it off. Sometimes it's impossible. And vacations? Well, you take them when you can get them."

"I know that," DeeDee said. "But couldn't you take a week off during the investigation?"

"DeeDee, to be honest I wouldn't be much fun to be around," Jake said. "I'd constantly be calling Al to find out what's happening, and I'd be thinking of the case all the time."

"You need to learn to switch it off."

"I couldn't agree with you more," he said. "Tell you what, though, we could definitely take a weekend vacation. I could switch off for two days."

"Great," DeeDee said. "We could go for a weekend city break."

"Sounds good to me," Jake said.

"Take in a show, maybe," DeeDee said. "Go out to eat. Go shopping. New York, perhaps? We could have a wintry weekend in style."

"Sounds expensive."

DeeDee sighed. "Okay, Mr. Killjoy. Tell you what, I'm going to pay for it, so you won't even know how much it costs. Susie and I will get another client like Tobias Crank, and we'll go celebrate in style.

"Honestly, we could go with the fee we got from catering his event, but I have it earmarked for savings and paying off the debts from some equipment we bought, plus some advertising I want to do to get these new clients. But the next big payday we have, we'll celebrate with a weekend vacation."

Jake grinned. "Sounds good to me. Now if you'll excuse me, I need to get back to my investigation."

"Happy sleuthing," DeeDee said. She looked at her phone and saw a couple of missed calls from a number she didn't recognize. When she returned the call, she discovered it was the Seattle Police Department, who wanted her to go in for an interview that afternoon at 2:00.

She spent the time until she had to leave for her appointment taking a long, luxurious bath, and then she took Yukon and Balto on a long walk along the edge of Puget Sound. It was nice to be close to nature, and she tried not to think about the investigation at all, although her mind inevitably wandered back to it.

When she returned, Jake had made a big late lunch of fried eggs, tomatoes, mushrooms, bacon, sausages, and tater tots. "This is much more filling than the tuna sandwich I was planning on making," DeeDee said as she ate. "Much more satisfying, too."

"After that exotic meal last night, figured you needed some down-home food," he said with a grin.

*****

A couple of hours later, she was back in Seattle in an interview room at the police station, waiting for someone to interview her.

Detective Kirton was fifteen minutes late when he finally arrived and didn't even offer an apology. He simply started the recording equipment and got down to business.

"DeeDee Wilson," he said. "Caterer at Deelish."

"Yes," she said.

"Who hired you to cater the event?"

"Tobias Crank, the director of the opera."

"Yes, I'm well aware who Tobias Crank is."

DeeDee struggled not to raise an eyebrow at his tone, but managed to stay calm and composed.

"This news is about to be released to the public, so I might as well tell you. Angel Bridges was murdered." He watched her reaction carefully.

"I see."

"The autopsy showed she was poisoned. A broken champagne glass was found next to her, so it's likely the poison was in the champagne."

"Oh no!" DeeDee said. "Poor woman."

"You, your colleague, and your waiters had access to the champagne in the kitchen, and you personally were not present in the dining room during the meal, which gave you an opportunity to hand the glass to Angel Bridges."

DeeDee felt like her heart had stopped. "You're not… accusing me?"

"I'm asking questions. It's my job."

"So what question is it that you're asking me?"

"If you handed her the glass with poison in it."

"No, of course not!"

He watched her, his eyes unblinking and very unnerving.

"Why would I do something like that?" she asked, her face becoming hot. "What possible motive could I have had? I didn't even know her apart from seeing her on TV and in movies."

"Maybe you did it for someone else. Maybe someone paid you to do it."

"No."

"Tobias Crank paid you a huge sum of money for your catering services. Far above the average fee for such services. Why?"

"Because he wanted us to do something special."

"Something like murder?"

DeeDee was starting to get angry. "Are you suggesting I use my catering business as a front for my hitman services? Or is it an added extra? A five-course meal with hors d'oeuvre and some poison on the side, if you're willing to pay an extra two thousand bucks?"

"You tell me."

"I'm telling you the very idea is ridiculous."

"This isn't the first time someone's been murdered at an event you've catered."

DeeDee swallowed. "I know. But it was just bad luck."

"We'll see," he said with a menacing look in his eye. "We'll see."

CHAPTER EIGHT

As soon as DeeDee left the interview with Detective Kirton, she called Jake to tell him what had happened and then she called Susie. She was walking back to the parking lot, and her hand was shaking as she held her phone.

"I can't believe it," she said to Susie. "He was trying to say maybe we had something to do with this."

"What?" Susie said, shocked. "How?"

DeeDee explained what had gone on in the interview room. "I find it a very strange way of investigating. When are you going in for an interview?"

"I haven't been called yet," Susie said. "Don't worry. I'll tell him very firmly we had nothing to do with it. As for Tobias paying caterers to kill his leading lady? It seems Kirton has been reading too many far-fetched murder mysteries."

"I agree," DeeDee said. "But I'm still feeling angry about it. Thankfully Al and Cassie are coming over tonight, so I've got that to look forward to. You're welcome to come, too, if you'd like."

"I'd love to," Susie said. "But I'm washing my hair." She laughed. "Just kidding. My mom's coming in from out of town, so I'll be here with her."

DeeDee sighed. "Well, at least you can keep your sense of humor. That's crucial in stressful times. I just can't believe he'd even think of something that crazy, let alone mention it."

"It's laughable, nothing more," Susie said firmly. "We need to keep a positive attitude and keep in mind how laughable it is."

But Tobias Crank certainly wasn't laughing when he called DeeDee that evening. In fact, he sounded like he'd been crying. DeeDee pictured him striding back and forth in his enormous apartment, with red eyes and a worried, pale face.

"Tobias?" DeeDee said. She was cleaning the kitchen when he called in preparation for cooking dinner for Al and Cassie.

"I'm so sorry to bother you," he said. "I... well..."

For a man who was normally so articulate, his stuttering speech was disconcerting. "What's the matter?"

"I just came back from my interview at the police station."

"I see," she said. "So Detective Kirton made up a wild story about you, too?"

"Yes," he said. "It was totally and completely unfounded. I am not a murderer. I am so far from being a murderer it's ridiculous. I would not steal a piece of candy, let alone poison someone."

"I'm sure you wouldn't," DeeDee said. For some reason, she really believed him.

He paused. "You don't think I did it, do you?"

"No," DeeDee said. "Gut feeling."

"Well, that's a relief, because..." He trailed off.

"Because…?"

"Because you mentioned your husband was a private investigator. I want him to investigate this to make sure I have something to offer in case the police go ahead and mistakenly charge me. Detective Kirton said my fingerprints were found on shards of the champagne glass Angel had been holding, and he's going to do whatever it takes to nail me."

"Oh, no."

"Yes. It doesn't look good for me. But I didn't do it, honestly, I didn't. Perhaps I'm being framed. All I know is that I need someone on my side, and I don't know anyone in this town. Do you think your husband will do it?"

Jake was at the store buying ingredients for their dinner that night. "He's out right now," DeeDee said. "As soon as he returns, I'll talk to him and he'll get back to you."

"Thank you," Tobias said. "Please try to persuade him. I hate to use such a crude term, but I really am desperate. And in terms of money, don't worry. You know Mr. Marks will pay whatever you need and more. This production sinks without me, and I'm certain that Mr. Marks will do anything to make sure that doesn't happen."

"Okay, sure," DeeDee said. "I'll see what I can do." She paused before she hung up. "I'm so sorry this is happening, Tobias."

"So am I," he said and ended the call.

Within a few minutes, Jake walked into the kitchen with a grocery bag filled with tuna steaks and vegetables, singing to himself.

"I can tell you're happy," DeeDee said with a smile.

"I had some Aerosmith playing in the car," he said. "Trying to relieve the stress, and it worked like a charm." He walked over to her, handed her the bag of groceries, and kissed her.

"I hope this won't burst your bubble, but the experience Tobias had with Detective Kirton was similar to mine. He's worried the murder is going to be pinned on him. Kirton said his fingerprints were on the broken champagne glass. Tobias thinks he's being framed, and Kirton seems determined to get enough evidence to charge him with murder, and by the way, it has now been officially confirmed that it is murder. Angel was poisoned."

"This Kirton sounds unnecessarily aggressive," Jake said. "That is, unless Tobias really did it."

"I'm sure he didn't, Jake," DeeDee said. "It's a gut feeling thing. He wants you to help him prove his innocence."

Jake had walked over to the kitchen table to put his papers in his briefcase, but he paused and looked up. "Really?"

"Yes," DeeDee said. "He has a generous benefactor who will pay all the costs. The problem is, I know you're busy with the Jessup case."

"Yes."

"Too busy?"

Jake looked like he was giving it serious consideration. "Well... Yes, really. But given what Kirton said to you earlier today, I think we should stay involved. That way you've got protection if he comes after you. We'll find out the truth, and he won't be able to refute it."

DeeDee nodded. "I'm sure he won't be able to come after me. There won't be any evidence. But even so, it sounds like a good idea, sort of like buying some insurance."

"The only thing is timing," he said. "We're going to be short on time given my involvement in the Jessup case. Unless..."

"Unless?"

"You wouldn't want to put your investigating skills to the test again, would you?"

"You want me to take on the case?"

"Jointly," he said. "I know you're busy with your catering business, so you couldn't do it full time. But maybe if I do part time, and you do part time, we just might be able to crack it."

DeeDee paused. "You might just be right. All right, I'll do it."

"However, there's one thing to think about."

"Which is?"

"We need payment up front," Jake said. "Because this 'generous benefactor' isn't going to be paying if we find out it was Tobias who did it."

DeeDee thought back to the slow, smooth, charming Lowell Marks. "I'm sure if we found out Tobias did it, Marks would offer us whatever we wanted to pin it on someone else. You know, plant evidence, do whatever we had to."

Jake sighed. "Another set of shady characters to deal with? I've got enough of those in the Jessup case."

"Obviously, we wouldn't take the deal," DeeDee said.

"And then what?" Jake said. "He might send people to come and make us take the deal. Those types always have something up their sleeve, and they don't take no for an answer. They have too much money and too much power. They will do whatever they have to do to get their way."

DeeDee nodded. "Well, I think that's a chance we'll have to take," she said. "I'd bet our house Tobias didn't do it, and, like you said, finding out who did do it protects me as well."

"Yes," Jake said. "That's the main reason I want to do it, to protect you."

"And Susie," DeeDee said. "I expect Detective Kirton will have similar things to say to her. Similar ridiculous accusations."

"Okay, let's do it," Jake said. "Let's get Al and Cassie involved, too. The more minds we have on it, the better."

"I agree," DeeDee said. "Now I need to fix a delicious dinner to persuade them."

"And I'll make sure the house is thoroughly acceptable while you're doing that."

The house was inviting, and the delicious smell of seared tuna steaks with garlic filled their home. DeeDee took two cooked pieces of tuna steak, and gave one each to Yukon and Balto. It was one of their favorites. Privately, DeeDee wondered if the husky breed had a little cat thrown in it.

*****

Al and Cassie arrived and soon the four of them were sitting at the kitchen table, clinking their glasses together and enjoying the wonderful meal DeeDee had prepared. Through the large window, they had a perfect view of the evening shadows as they settled in over Puget Sound. It was truly gorgeous. It was just a shame the subject matter of their discussions wasn't as relaxing.

Thankfully, when they'd filled Al and Cassie in on everything that had happened with Angel's murder, they enthusiastically jumped on board right away and accepted Jake and DeeDee's request to help with the investigation into the murder of Angel Bridges.

"Ain't 'bout to let some jumped-up detective throw ya' behind bars, DeeDee," Al said. "Not when ya' cook for us like this. I'd miss yer' dinners too much."

"Perhaps you could get up and say that in court," DeeDee said, glad she was able to add a little humor to the situation. "They find me guilty and are about to send me away for life, but they spare me because if I am not there to cook, the three of you will starve."

Al chuckled again. "Ya' can call it 'acquitted on compassionate grounds.'"

"Stop it, you two," Cassie said. "Now, you've said you know Tobias Crank and that British guy who left the room during dinner. You said some women left too, but you're not sure which women."

"Yes, the waitress who told me wasn't sure."

"Do you think she'd know them if she saw a picture of them?"

"Maybe," DeeDee said.

"Well, we'll just pull all the women's pictures off the website for the *Akhnaten* opera and see if she recognizes any of them."

"I like that idea," DeeDee said. "That would be a good start. And we can go talk to Tobias and Laurence and see if they know anything about who left the room. That will give us a good reason for visiting them, actually investigating them, without letting them know that's what we're doing."

Cassie clinked her glass with DeeDee's. "There's a plan. We should set up our own investigating firm. We don't need these two bozos cramping our style." They all laughed.

"And I'm expecting payment for this, you two," Cassie said nodding at Al and Jake. "And DeeDee gets paid, too. The two of us are on the payroll starting right now, darling. Let's have expensive lunches and charge them back to the business. What do you say, DeeDee?"

DeeDee laughed. "Speaking of which, did you know that Al and Jake are taking one of the men they're investigating to Canlis, of all places?"

"Well, I can't judge them too harshly for that. Any excuse to go to Canlis is a good one." She winked at DeeDee. "And I'm sure we'll be able to find a good excuse to go there at some point."

DeeDee laughed. "When we wrap up this investigation, why don't we all go?"

"Depends how it goes with l'il Joshy Jessup," Al said. "If it don't go well, Ima not gonna' wanna' go back there. That's fer sure."

"Ever the drama lama," Cassie said with a laugh. "I'm sure it'll go just fine, darling."

"I'm sure it will, too," DeeDee said.

"I hope so," Jake added.

"The four of us don't go out together often enough," Cassie said. "Which gives me an idea. Why don't we all go see *Akhnaten*? We may be able to catch some of the players by the stage door, and we can investigate them while we talk to them. Or, you never know, watching it might give us some clues. Who knows what we might pick up?"

"If ya' wanna' see the opera, jes' say so and I'll take ya, Cassie," Al said. "Long as ya' don't mind me snorin' all the way through it."

"Consider it part of your cultural education," Cassie said.

Al put his fork down. "Ya' sure got a tongue on ya' tonight, my little viper."

"All right, all right," Cassie said, laughing. "How about 'It would be so wonderful for you to learn about the opera, my darling Philistine.' That better?" Her eyes twinkled as she looked at him.

He nodded at Jake. "This woman'll be the death of me."

"She's the life of you, my friend, and you well know it," Jake said.

"Yeah, yer' right," Al said as he blew Cassie a kiss across the table.

Cassie got out her phone. "Sorry to be so unmannerly at the dinner table, but let's book this opera." She winked at DeeDee. "And charge it to the business expense account. You boys coming?"

"I'm up for it," Jake said. "It'll be my first time at the opera."

"First fer me too," Al said. "And probably my last."

"Oh my gosh!" DeeDee said. "I've just remembered something. I can't believe I forgot this! All the shock and the late night must have gotten to me."

Jake leaned forward on his elbows. "What is it?"

DeeDee grimaced. "I think you guys are going to kill me."

Al looked at Jake and Cassie. "Got my Mac-10 in my waistband, in case we gotta' take her out."

"Even I know that big of a gun couldn't be hidden in your waistband, but don't even joke about something like that," Cassie said. Concealed weapons were a sensitive subject with her, because of Al's Mafia past.

"Sorry," Al said contritely.

"Tobias and Angel were having an argument last night."

"About what?" Jake gently asked.

"He was saying she needed to follow his direction. She told him she got him a seventeen-minute standing ovation. He said that was more due to Laurence than her. He said he'd be getting rid of her at the end of the season, and she said to make sure it was the end of the season and not before, since they have a contract and if he breaks it…" Her heart sank. "There would be very expensive consequences. That's a motive."

Jake leaned back in his chair. "It is, indeed. That plus his fingerprints on the glass shard? And the fact he left the dining room during dinner? DeeDee, that could even be enough to get him charged for her murder."

"Oh man, how could I have forgotten that?" DeeDee scolded herself. "Maybe he did it, after all. We can't take this case because of a conflict of interest, can we?"

"I don't think so," Jake said quietly.

"Wrongo!" Al said. "We get Daddy Warbucks to pay us a bundle, then if it is this Crank guy, we give the info back to the cops. That way we ain't done nothin' illegal since we're gonna' be hired and paid by Daddy Warbucks, not Crank."

Jake twisted his mouth. "I don't know. It's a close call on the conflicts issue, but it sure would be good to keep our foot in the door in case Kirton tries to charge DeeDee."

"I say let's do it," Cassie said. "Just get the payment for the services up front, DeeDee."

"Okay, I will," DeeDee said. "Are you all sure you want to go through with this?"

"Sure as sure," Al said.

"Yes," Jake said. "But for you, not for Tobias Crank."

"I'm in," Cassie said.

DeeDee smiled, feeling surrounded by love. "Thanks, guys."

CHAPTER NINE

DeeDee called Tobias Crank back to let him know they were prepared to take the case, and he insisted on having a meeting with DeeDee and Jake at his apartment. Lowell Marks would be there to sign the check, a very large check.

They met with Lowell and Tobias, and while DeeDee had wanted to question Tobias about his argument with Angel, Lowell Marks made her feel so uncomfortable she could barely say anything. He had this air of authority that dwarfed everything and everyone in the room, as if he was the only person there.

At the end of the meeting, Lowell Marks took Jake's hand, and said in a low tone, almost a whisper, "Do the right thing."

When DeeDee and Jake got into the elevator, they gave each other a meaningful look.

"Do the right thing?" DeeDee said. "That sounds to me like, make sure Tobias isn't implicated."

"That it does," Jake said. "If Detective Kirton hadn't mentioned the idea of you being involved, I'd turn around right now and give him back his check."

"We still can," DeeDee said. "I'm sure the truth will come out, because I'm innocent, and I have nothing to hide."

Jake grimaced. "I wish the police force and the legal system worked that way. But when it comes to someone's day in court, it's not about truth or justice. It's about which side can tell the most convincing story. And sometimes, I hate to say, it comes down to which side knows the most influential people."

"I know you're right," DeeDee said. "There have been enough innocent people convicted over the years for me to see that."

"And enough guilty people who've gotten away scot-free."

DeeDee nodded. "That, too. Well, let's find out who did this, and have irrefutable evidence ready."

"I agree."

"That will save my behind, and Tobias', if his deserves saving."

"Time will tell," Jake said. "We'll soon find out."

"Yes," DeeDee said. "For now, go back to working on the Jessup case, and I'll talk to Susie so we can figure out how we can pull in some new clients. We're going to the opera tomorrow, so let's hang tight until then and give ourselves a break. What do you say?"

"Good idea," Jake said. "I have to dive into more research on Jessup, so the break will do me good. We can come back to it with refreshed minds, too, which should help us come up with more ideas. Maybe we can pick up on some little things we missed."

The break did do them good.

*****

By the time their opera excursion rolled around, DeeDee was feeling much more relaxed. The morning of the opera, Jake discovered that Joshua Jessup had a police arrest record for possession and intent to supply cocaine, and yet he'd never even been charged.

"I'm guessing Daddy paid it off," Jake said. He grinned for the rest of the day. That was the type of information he'd been looking for, controversy-sparking information.

While they were both in a very good mood, the same couldn't be said of Cassie and Al. The atmosphere was rather frosty when Jake and DeeDee got into the car. Cassie had come out of the front seat, rather too angrily, and got in the back to sit next to DeeDee, so the two men could sit up front. They both stared resolutely forward.

Cassie looked absolutely beautiful. She wore a red dress, her hair was in an updo, and her makeup had been applied immaculately. But her red lipsticked mouth was a thin angry line.

"What's going on?" DeeDee whispered as they drove off.

"Nothing," Cassie said quietly. "Don't worry about it."

DeeDee gave her a knowing look as if to say, "It's me, come on!"

Thankfully the guys started talking about other things, boating, to be precise, so Cassie and DeeDee could talk quietly without being overheard.

"Come on, what's up?" DeeDee asked.

Cassie sighed and looked at her for the first time since DeeDee and Jake had gotten in the car. "I'm sorry. You look wonderful, by the way."

"Thank you," DeeDee said. She really did. Normally for such an occasion she'd have opted for a dress, but wide leg high-waisted pantsuits with matching cropped jackets in a light silk that flowed were in fashion, and she'd taken the plunge and bought one. It had an Aztec pattern in cream, gold, teal, and orange, and looked absolutely wonderful with her teal high heels. "But that's not important. What's going on with you and Al?"

"Ugh. DeeDee, I thought I was fine with him continuing to do private investigating. But this case seems so dangerous. I thought he'd left the dangerous life behind him, after all that happened when he was in the mob. But he seems to like the danger. Did you know they found out that someone at the company, a guy who was a potential whistleblower, was found dead in his apartment? I expect Jake told you."

DeeDee paused. "No, he didn't. When was this? Recently?"

"No, a few years back," DeeDee said. "But it shows they're prepared to kill. What if it was that Joshua Jessup guy who did it, because he was going to be exposed? And now Al's going to go in there and talk about Joshua's cocaine issues or whatever and get the guy riled up. How does he know the guy isn't going to come after him? Or me? Or my kids?"

DeeDee didn't know how to answer her. Why hadn't Jake told her? Because he didn't want to worry her? Even if that was the case, even with all the noble sentiment behind it, she wouldn't have been happy. She didn't want protecting.

If Jake was in a difficult situation, she wanted to support him through it, not be left in the dark because she 'couldn't handle it.' She found it disrespectful, like she was some little woman who could only handle catering jobs.

But Jake hadn't been like that before. He'd always confided in her. So why not this time?

"Let's just forget about it for tonight," DeeDee said. "Let's focus on this investigation. We can deal with all of that later."

"If there even is a later," Cassie said. "I don't for the life of me know why he wants to put himself in all these dangerous situations. Why can't he be, I don't know, a landscape designer, or a wine critic, or a travel writer? There are a millions of career options that don't have the propensity to turn fatal. Why doesn't he just pick one of those?"

"You're angry," DeeDee soothed. "I know, and I understand. Quite frankly, I'm not feeling the greatest right now either, based on what you just told me, that Jake hasn't even let me know. This is the first I've heard of it. But please, let's just try to put it to the side for now and be focused. We need to be thinking clearly and on our A-game at *Akhnaten* tonight. If we're angry and not thinking straight, we very well may miss clues."

Cassie sighed again. "You're right. Okay. Sorry for making this all about me. It's just that it feels so unsafe."

"It's okay," DeeDee said. "Totally understandable."

Cassie leaned over and gave her a quick hug. Then she shook her head, like she was trying to shake the anger away, and managed to smile. "Right. My investigator hat is firmly on!"

They had to park a little ways from the theater in a parking garage and enjoyed the walk to the Seattle Opera House. The breeze off the Sound was cold and the street was filled with people, but not to the extent they didn't feel safe.

DeeDee managed to put her feelings aside and linked her arm with Jake's as they walked. Cassie did the same with Al, although she did throw DeeDee a dirty look. DeeDee smirked.

"So," DeeDee said, trying to get rid of the slightly awkward atmosphere that hovered around them. "It's your first time, Jake, and your first time, Al. This is my second time, but the first time was when I was a teenager, so that doesn't really count. Since Cassie is a seasoned opera-goer, I'm sure she'll keep us all up to speed with what's going on."

"I looked it up," Cassie said. "It's being sung in Hebrew, Egyptian and Akkadian, which is most unusual."

"How in the heck are we gonna' understand it?" Al asked.

"You're not," Cassie said. "They project the translation into

English above the stage."

"I see," Jake said. "It's kind of like a foreign film. You have to read your way through the opera."

Cassie grinned. "'Fraid so. My, my, I'm getting the sense that the two of you aren't taking this with good sportsmanship."

"I didn't mean anything by it," Jake said. "We're here more to see if we can find something out about Angel Bridges' murder, rather than the opera itself."

"Yes," DeeDee said, trying not to feel annoyed. "That's why we're here too." *So now Jake was hiding his own investigation from her and trying to take over hers, too?* She knew it was probably an uncharitable thought, but under the circumstances, justified.

There wasn't much more to be said, so they were all silent as they entered the opera house, checked their coats, and went to get a glass of champagne. Cassie ate olive after olive from the bar, and it didn't seem that her mood had changed.

"C'mon guys," Al said. "Gotta' make a toast. Let's all put on a happy face. Why are we all so miserable, huh? Our careers are all goin' great, we got two cases we're doin', and DeeDee's takin' her caterin' business to new heights. I'd say that's pretty good."

"I didn't hear you mention my career," Cassie said tightly.

Al paused, then chuckled. "Oh, but darlin' yer' always doin' good. You'll out-earn and outclass the rest of us for yer' whole career. Sorry, Jake. Sorry, DeeDee."

"And now you go and insult our friends," Cassie said. She looked like she was about to cry.

DeeDee decided to take control of the situation. "Here," she said, grabbing Cassie's drink and handing it to Al, then handing her own champagne flute to Jake. "One moment, please. We'll be back soon."

She ushered Cassie to the ladies room.

"Seriously, come on!" DeeDee said, taking her by the shoulders. "I know you're upset, but please, Cassie, pull yourself together. I need you to be strong right now. I really do."

Just then, a young woman came stalking into the bathroom in high heels, flicking her long brown hair and talking on a Bluetooth headset. DeeDee still hadn't quite gotten used to those things. It looked like people were walking down the street talking to themselves.

"Honestly? I can't believe they're still even going to have the show after what happened to Angel Bridges. It's all over the news here. Is it like that with you? Well, of course she was like, super-famous. I'm here to check out who's playing her role now."

"Think about it, that's probably the person who killed her. You know, the cover who now has the main part." She laughed at something the other person said. "Yeah! I'll bet that's why half the people are here tonight. It's like really busy."

Cassie had stopped snivelling and was looking directly at DeeDee. She raised her eyebrows. When the woman had left, Cassie said, "Too obvious? Or do you think she might have a point?"

"Well, it wasn't that obvious, since we didn't think of it."

"True. You know what we need to do?" Cassie started scrambling in her purse. "We need to write down a list of all the people it could possibly be, and why."

DeeDee laughed. "Also known as suspects and motives."

"Oh, all right, Ms. Technical. So, Tobias Crank is at the top of the list because he wanted out of the contract." She got a notepad out of her purse and began to write on it.

"Yes," DeeDee said, shifting from one foot to the other

nervously. She still felt a little embarrassed about overhearing Tobias and Angel. "Laurence Powers, because they were always arguing."

"Yes…" Cassie said, furiously writing. "And whoever the cover for Angel is, just like that glamorous woman said. Who else?"

"The women Tanya said had left the table during dinner when she was in the dining room serving dinner. We'll have to get in touch with her and show her the pictures from the opera program, to see if she knows who it might have been."

"Fine," Cassie said, writing Random Women – Tanya.

"That's all we've got right now," DeeDee said. She put her hand out. "I'll keep it safe."

"Okay."

"Sorry for being so silly," Cassie said. "It was all just getting to me. I'm feeling quite hormonal at the moment as well. Ugh. I'm sorry. I promise I'll be 100% focused on working out who did this to Angel Bridges."

"Thanks," DeeDee said. "And don't worry. Let's just stay on track."

Cassie flashed her a wicked grin. "Let's go and see which primadonna has taken over the role of Nefertiti. Who knows, she may just be our killer."

"Maybe," DeeDee said. She got her lipstick out of her purse and began to reapply it. "It seems a little extreme, though, to go to such lengths for a part."

"You haven't seen that movie *All About Eve,* have you? You know, the one with Bette Davis? The girl in it is insane, and does all kinds of devious and unethical things to get a part in a play. She could have easily stretched to murder. And if someone wanted a part that badly, they just might have."

CHAPTER TEN

Before the opera began, Tobias Crank came out on stage and made an unexpected speech. He looked even more gloriously eccentric than usual with his fitted green velvet suit and gold jewelry. DeeDee, Jake, Cassie, and Al watched him from their box on the right-hand side of the theater.

"Ladies and gentlemen," he began. "I'm sure you're all aware by now that our wonderful and talented leading lady, Angel Bridges, who played the part of Nefertiti, has passed away. Unfortunately, she was murdered."

You could have heard a pin drop in the audience.

He began to walk back and forth across the stage in front of the curtain. "Angel and I had our artistic differences, but we were brought together, for a far too short time, by our love of opera. Honestly, ladies and gentlemen, I was thinking of canceling the rest of the performances in her honor. I thought it would be too painful for all of us to go on.

"But then I had a change of heart. I thought we must carry on, beautifully, elegantly, and gracefully, with Angel's spirit guiding us. Oh, how appropriate her name is now! Angel Bridges. Our Angel has crossed over the bridge to the afterlife to be with the other angels. And now she looks down on us.

"So we are going to put on the most spectacular show we possibly can, in her memory. And we will continue doing so, night after night after night, for Angel."

Everyone in the theater applauded.

He let the applause continue for some time, then he held up his hand. "I want to mention Angel's husband, Julius, who is in the audience with us tonight. Julius, we extend our most sincere condolences to you, and can only hope that our small offering of this performance will bring you a bit of comfort in this difficult time.

"We wish we could do more, but we as humble performers can only seek to create fleeting beauty, which binds our hearts together for mere moments. We sincerely wish we could take the pain of the human condition and its depravity away. But rather, we can only document it in stories that are more real than reality itself. So that we all, in our moments of pain and suffering, know that we are not alone.

"With that said, I present to you, *Akhnaten*."

He disappeared behind the curtain, and the music began.

DeeDee was surprisingly moved by Tobias Crank's speech. She found herself thinking that someone with that level of sensitivity and artistry could not be capable of murder.

She whispered as much to Cassie, who sighed and said, "I wish that was true, but maybe it makes them more likely to do something like commit murder. I mean all those emotions constantly bubbling up in them make them perfect candidates for crimes of passion, like killing in fits of rage."

"Maybe," DeeDee said. "But poisoning isn't that type of a crime. It's cold, calculated, and premeditated. I just can't see him doing that."

Cassie shrugged. "Maybe you're right."

DeeDee had bought a program and studied it before Tobias Crank had come onto the stage and the auditorium lights had been dimmed. She knew Nefertiti didn't appear on stage until the last scene of the first act, so they had quite a while to wait. The programs hadn't been changed yet, except for a gold sticker that had been stuck on the front with a picture of Angel Bridges. RIP was written above it with tributes below. Inside the program, under Nefertiti, Angel Bridges' name was still listed.

Lola Newman was listed as her cover. Her headshot was stunning She was a very pretty young woman with a long sweep of thick blonde hair cascading over her shoulders. DeeDee felt strange, not knowing whether she was staring into the perfectly made-up face of a killer, or a perfectly innocent opera singer. Everything felt uncertain right now.

In the first act there was a funeral scene with hammering drums. The program said it was King Aye singing. DeeDee didn't recognize the man and hadn't been introduced to him at the party. She wondered if he'd attended it, and if not, why not.

But what Tanya had said really stuck in her mind, and she was more focused on women, the women who left the dining room that night and who might have potentially killed Angel.

DeeDee anxiously awaited the third scene. Not only would Nefertiti be coming onstage, but so would Queen Tiye. DeeDee recognized the picture listed for Queen Tiye in the program. It was the older lady, Siobhan Whitehead, the one who had been so kind to DeeDee and interested in her catering business. DeeDee had warmed up to her, but she made a promise to herself that she wouldn't let her feelings get in the way of the investigation.

The scene was very rousing, with Laurence, Lola Newman, and Queen Tiye all singing together. Then the curtain went down and the lights in the auditorium went up.

"Wow," DeeDee said, stunned. She ran her hand over her arm. "I've got goosebumps from that."

"Now that's what I call a performance," Al said, beaming. "I wanna' do this again, Cassie. Mattera' fact I'll come to the opera every month if ya' want."

Cassie smiled at him, seeming to have dropped her earlier angry feelings. "Maybe once every three months. If you came every month it wouldn't seem so special. What did you think of it, Jake?"

"Not as bad as I thought it would be," Jake said. "I think I'll stick to my rock music, but it was interesting enough. Those people can really sing, though, huh?"

"Ya' don't say," Al said, nudging him in the ribs and rolling his eyes at the women.

"Queen Tiye was especially good," Cassie said.

"Yes, and she was lovely when I met her at the opening night party," DeeDee said. "That said, I still have to investigate her. Remember Tanya said some women she didn't recognize left the room. Maybe she's one of them. I'll take the program over to Tanya and see if she remembers. But even if she doesn't recognize Siobhan, I think I'll still talk to her. She might have seen something, know something."

"Okay," Cassie said. "She's going on the list."

"Any possible motive?" Jake asked.

"Not that I can think of," DeeDee said. "Maybe she's jealous of Angel Bridges stealing the spotlight, but I can't see what she'd have to gain by murdering her. She's too old to be cast as Nefertiti, so it can't be that."

They went out during the intermission to get drinks. Al was driving so he didn't have another drink. Jake and Cassie each had a glass of champagne and DeeDee opted for a glass of orange juice. She knew if she drank any more her mind would get fuzzy, and she needed to be as sharp as possible.

"One second," she said, since she wanted to go to the bathroom. There was a ridiculously long line for the ladies' restrooms which snaked out into the lobby.

She sighed, but it turned out to be a good thing, since it allowed her to catch sight of a most unwelcome figure drinking at the bar. It took her a moment to recognize him, but her stomach had already dropped and her legs felt heavy, letting her know it was certainly not someone she wanted to see. Then, in a flash, it came back to her. It was Detective Kirton.

DeeDee left her place in the line and hurried back to Cassie, Jake, and Al. "Detective Kirton's here," she said. Her heart was racing. Objectively, she knew there was nothing to worry about. He wasn't going to break out the cuffs and drag her screaming to jail, but that didn't stop her palms from sweating and her breath from tightening in her throat. "What do you think he's doing here?"

"Whoa, take a breath," Jake said, coming over and rubbing her on the back. "Actually, take several breaths."

"Don't worry," Cassie said. "He's probably just doing exactly what we are, immersing himself in the opera world to see if he can find more clues and see if he can figure out what's going on."

DeeDee took a long deep breath. "You're right. I know you're right. That guy, ugh, he just gives me the heebie jeebies."

Jake looked frustrated. "You know what? I think I should call Dan. I've been thinking about it for a couple of days."

Dan Hewson was the chief of police, and a friend of Jake's.

"No," DeeDee said. "Please don't. I mean, what would you say to him?"

"I'd tell him about the way this so-called 'detective' treated you when you were called in for questioning."

DeeDee shook her head. "Fine, but what's he going to do? If he tells Kirton about it, Kirton's only going to have it in even more for me. Trust me, the last thing I want to do right now is draw negative attention to myself."

"Yeah," Jake said. "I know what you mean. But maybe he can just keep an eye on him."

"I don't know," DeeDee said. "He might tell us to leave the investigation alone and say it's a police matter, or whatever. I just don't get a good feeling about it, Jake."

"Okay" Jake said, then he sighed. "I don't know. I just hate seeing you this way."

DeeDee softened and leaned into him. "I know, darling, but I was just having an off moment. I'll be fine, honest. If things get really bad, we'll call Dan. But for now, we can handle it ourselves." She smiled at all of them. "We're a great team, right?"

Cassie linked arms with her. "That we are. We can do this. Tell you what, let's sneak out of the performance when they're doing all the clapping at the end. It usually goes on for ages. Then we can be the first ones by the stage door, and we'll see if we can corner anyone."

Al laughed. "Better watch out ya' don't get charged with harassment, Cass."

CHAPTER ELEVEN

Unfortunately, their stage door attempt was very disappointing. They weren't the only ones near the stage doors. There were numerous reporters crowding around. "Obviously they're trying to get the scoop from the insiders on the murder," DeeDee said.

For one thing, they couldn't get anywhere close to the doors. For another, when the players came out, they were rushed to their cars by security guards, so there was no opportunity to talk to anyone.

On the way home, DeeDee decided on their next plan of action. "I think we need to go talk to Lola Newman," she said to the other three. "She has a motive to get the part of Nefertiti. Cassie said I should have watched *All About Eve* to understand how treacherous people can be in order to get parts in showbusiness. I think she's a good place to start."

"I think so, too," Cassie said.

"I'll get in touch with Tobias and get the name, phone numbers and addresses of everyone in the cast. I expect many of them won't agree to talk to me. After all, I'm not a policeperson, so they don't have to. If they don't look amenable to talking to me, I might just pretend I'm trying to sell them my catering services."

"You'll do great," Jake said. "You can always make people tell you their secrets. You have a way about you that puts people at ease immediately."

"That's true," Cassie said, laughing. "And that's why you know everything about my life."

They all laughed.

The next morning, DeeDee started in earnest to investigate Angel's murder. Susie had sent her a text the night before to let her know they had a potential client in one of the wealthiest neighborhoods of Seattle.

Susie had said the client wanted to meet with them the following day and the meeting might last the entire day. As a result, she knew she had to get as much investigating done as she could today.

She called Tobias Crank first. "We were at the show last night and it was wonderful," she said. "You should be proud. I know Angel would be."

"Thank you," he replied, sounding choked up.

She asked for a list of the cast and crew, as well as their contact information, and he said that wouldn't be a problem. He told her he'd send it over by email. "We have a list for emergencies," he said, "so it's all here and ready for you. Really, I can't thank your husband enough for doing this."

"It's all right," she said. "We're glad to help."

"We...?" he asked.

"Yes, I'm helping him, given what Detective Kirton said to me."

"That man," Tobias said in disgust.

"I know," DeeDee said. "Don't even get me started. I'm going to go now, Tobias, before we go down that conversational road and my blood pressure goes through the roof."

He chuckled. "Sounds sensible. I'm going to go get some ice cream and calm myself down."

DeeDee smiled to herself. "Enjoy. I'm sure I'll be seeing you soon."

She walked Balto and Yukon for an hour, thinking about which member of the cast she'd target first. Eventually she settled on Lola Newman, because apart from Tobias, she was the only cast member who had a very strong motive.

DeeDee also made a note to call Tobias back at some point and ask for the contact information for Julius Bridges while he was in town. Historically, when a woman is murdered, quite often it turns out that it was their husband who did it. From the information she had, she knew he'd been out of town during the party.

But had he really been out of town? Could he have snuck into the apartment and poisoned his own wife? It seemed unlikely. But even if he wasn't responsible for her murder, since Angel probably talked to him about things the others wouldn't know, it was likely he might have some helpful information. In any event, it was worth going to talk to him and see what she could find out.

When she got home, she changed her clothes, put makeup on, and fed the dogs. Then she left for the ferry. While she was on it, she loaded the street address of where Lola Newman was staying into her GPS.

It took her into the center of the city and soon she was at the hotel. It had underground valet parking, which was a treat, so she handed over her keys and went inside. It was quite luxurious, and she thought Lowell Marks must have been the one financing her stay there.

DeeDee knew Lola was in room 123. She didn't want to ask for permission or have the receptionist call up to see if Lola would let her in, so she decided she'd have to use a little bit of subterfuge.

She walked across the gleaming marble floor, shoulders back and her chin held high, like she had all the confidence in the world.

"Hello," she said to the receptionist with a smile. "I'm here to see a friend. She's in room 123."

"Yes ma'am," the receptionist said with a smile. "The elevator is right there. Room 123 is on the first floor, so there's just one floor to go up."

"Thank you," DeeDee said, as she turned and walked towards the elevator.

"My pleasure," the receptionist said. "Have a great visit!"

DeeDee got into the elevator and went to the first floor, beginning to feel a little nervous. How was she going to start the conversation? She imagined Lola Newman opening the door to her, then wondering who on earth DeeDee was and what she was doing there.

After desperately racking her brain, an idea popped into her head, but it would only work if Lola was selfish and inconsiderate of Angel Bridges' death. The more DeeDee thought about it, the more she thought it might be a good way to find out how Lola really felt about Angel dying. She thought it might provide some insight into Lola's state of mind.

When DeeDee knocked on the door of room 123, her plan was firmly set in her mind.

A beautiful young woman with a sweep of blonde hair answered the door, a full face of makeup already applied. She didn't smile, and didn't look at all friendly. In fact, she frowned. "Who are you, again? You look vaguely familiar."

DeeDee fixed a smile on her face. "I'm DeeDee Wilson. I catered

Tobias Crank's party, the night, well, the night Angel Bridges was murdered."

A flicker of annoyance passed over Lola Newman's face. It looked like she'd hoped DeeDee was someone much more important or interesting. But then she smiled. "How may I help you?"

"I want to ask you something, but not here." DeeDee gestured around the hallway. "Someone might walk past and hear us."

Lola laughed in a carefree manner, but her eyes were clearly suspicious. "What could we possibly need to keep a secret?"

"It's not a secret," DeeDee said. "But I always like to be discreet when I can."

Lola looked her up and down, judging whether she should let her inside. "Okay. Come in."

The room was absolutely immaculate, the bed neatly made up, as if no one had even slept in it the night before. Lola was immaculate, too, with perfect nails, perfect hair, and a wearing a very stylish coordinated outfit. She gestured for DeeDee to sit on one of the chairs by the window. "I'm about to order breakfast," she said. "Would you like a coffee?"

"That would be great," DeeDee said. "An espresso or a cappuccino would be wonderful."

Lola smiled. "Certainly," she said. She placed her order on the phone, then sat on the edge of the bed and looked at DeeDee expectantly. "So…"

DeeDee swallowed. Now was the time for her to enact her plan. "Firstly, I want to congratulate you. You're now playing Nefertiti, and I saw your performance last night. It was absolutely stunning."

"Thank you," Lola said, a genuine smile crossing her face.

"Do you think there's any chance of Tobias keeping you on as Nefertiti now, instead of just filling in for Angel? Or is he hiring someone new? I think it would be such a shame if he did that, because you played the role so beautifully."

"I don't know," Lola said. A vein twitched on her forehead, but her smile never let up. "But thank you for your compliments."

"I was wondering… if you did get the part permanently, would you have a celebratory dinner? For your family, perhaps, or some of your fans?"

"Ah," Lola said. "So that's why you're here. I could be a potential customer."

DeeDee smiled guiltily. "I admit it," she said. "It's just that we so enjoyed catering the dinner for the opera people. It's the first time we've done it, and we found all of the cast members to be so accommodating."

"Well, normally I would have considered doing something like that," she said. "But since Angel Bridges has vacated the part due to being murdered, I don't think it would be appropriate." She smiled. "I'm a little surprised you asked, given the circumstances."

"Oh, I'm sorry, you're absolutely right," DeeDee said. "That really was very thoughtless of me."

"That's okay," Lola said graciously. "All of us are thoughtless from time to time." She smiled. "Will there be anything else?"

"No, that's all," DeeDee said. "Although my coffee hasn't come yet."

"Probably better to just leave it," Lola said.

The atmosphere was becoming a little awkward. "Yes."

Just then, there was a knock at the door. "Oh, if that's your coffee, you might as well drink it quickly," Lola said, going over to the door. But it wasn't the room service staff on the other side of the door. It was a man DeeDee didn't recognize.

"Julius Bridges?" Lola said, seemingly in shock. She looked back at DeeDee, then back to Julius. "What a surprise."

He looked upset, depressed, slightly tearful. His eyes flickered over to DeeDee. "Sorry to barge in on you like this."

DeeDee got up. "Not a problem. I was just leaving. My condolences to you, Mr. Bridges."

He wiped away a tear. "Thank you," he said. "I… I didn't know what I had until it was gone." He burst into tears, then quickly collected himself.

DeeDee had to think quickly. She knew this was probably the only time she would get to see Julius Bridges. How else was she going to contact him? But what to say…? Her mind raced. She thought about offering to cater the funeral, but that would only make her look crass and insensitive.

She walked slowly over to the door, desperately trying to think of what to say. Eventually, she landed on something. "It's such a terrible tragedy," she said. "I do hope the police have some leads…?"

"If they do, they haven't told me," Julius said.

"Oh, I see. Maybe you have some ideas of your own they could follow up on?"

He looked her straight in the eye and said, "Yes."

He was noticeably guarded. Lola stepped forward and said, "Julius, this is the caterer who did the food for the opening night party."

"Ah!" he said, his eyes shining. "If someone tampered with her drink, you'd have seen it, wouldn't you, in the kitchen?"

"I'm afraid not," DeeDee said. "The champagne was held outside the kitchen, in their own individual coolers."

"Right," he said tightly, as if she should have been keeping a closer eye on a potential poisoning situation she hadn't even known existed. But she could understand his thinking. "Well…"

He clearly wanted her to leave.

"I'll be going now," she said. "Thank you for your time, Lola."

"Bye, now!" Lola said with a smile and cheery wave. She was obviously very glad to see the back of DeeDee.

As soon as DeeDee was in the parking garage waiting for the valet to bring her car around, she called Susie and explained what happened. "There's something not sitting right with me. Why would Julius Bridges be visiting Lola?"

"To have an affair, of course," Susie said. "They've always been lovers, and they killed Angel to get Lola the part and get rid of her, so they can be together."

DeeDee sighed. "I think you've been reading too many murder mysteries. Let's try to look for innocent explanations first. Maybe it was because Lola was playing Nefertiti, he wanted to personally thank her for such a great performance in place of Angel? Or maybe he thinks they were close and just wants to be near the people who were working with Angel."

"Maybe, I guess," Susie said, sounding a little deflated.

"By the way, he told me that the police don't have any leads."

"That's good."

"Why?" DeeDee asked.

"It means they're not investigating Tobias, you, or me. That Detective Kirton is a real piece of work, but it looks like he was only bluffing."

"Yes, thank goodness," DeeDee said. "Though I wouldn't be surprised if he had some tricks up his sleeve." She sighed. "Well, I'm going to head back to Bainbridge Island now. I'll try and get some rest, so I'll be fresh for our potential client tomorrow. My head is killing me."

"Yes, you do need to rest up for this one," Susie said. "It could be one of our biggest jobs yet, and she's very well connected, so she could put us in touch with tons of new clients, too."

"Sounds good," DeeDee said. She was having trouble getting excited about it, and that was a clear sign to her she really did need to get some rest.

CHAPTER TWELVE

DeeDee had fallen asleep just before 8:00 the evening before, so when she awoke the following morning at 6:00, she was feeling refreshed and ready for the day. She took Balto and Yukon on a long walk, then made a big breakfast spread for Jake and her of yogurt, fresh fruit, and croissants with cheese and bacon.

Susie had given her instructions on how to dress. She'd been told to "dress nice, but not evening dress nice," so she put on one of her outfits she wore when she needed to look sophisticated, but still casual. It was a matching top and slacks, in a wonderful rose pink color.

They were wide leg slacks, a style she wore well and was really glad had come back in vogue. The top had a couple of little ruffles which made it feminine, but not too fussy. She accented the outfit with a loose wavy hairstyle, block high heels in gray and her most expensive purse, a gray and white designer one Jake had bought for her. Silver jewelry completed the look. Susie wanted them to dress to impress this client, and DeeDee thought her ensemble would work.

They decided to meet at a coffee shop and go over their presentation, then DeeDee would drive them to the client's house in Seattle. "Because your car is nicer," was how Susie had put it.

Privately, DeeDee thought it didn't matter all that much what they wore or what car they drove. Their job was to cater, but she understood what Susie was doing, so she went along with it.

When they met at the coffee shop, Susie looked like she'd just come from the beauty salon and wore a dress, blazer, and high heels.

"Wow, you look glamorous," DeeDee said.

"Thanks," Susie said, grinning. "As do you. I'm going to put my salon charge on my expense account."

"Just this once," DeeDee said with a smile.

They ordered their coffees and sat down.

"So," DeeDee said, sipping her cappuccino. "What about this client has you so on edge?"

"It's not a client, it's a potential client," Susie said. "We can't afford to get ahead of ourselves."

"All right, a potential client."

Susie took a deep breath. "It's a wedding. But no ordinary wedding. Our potential client's daughter is marrying some duke from England, and guess how many guests they've invited? A thousand! We'd be catering for a thousand guests."

"Whoa," DeeDee said.

"They're one of the wealthiest families in Seattle. I heard through the grapevine that the duke doesn't have anything, so it's like one of those old convenience marriages, you know? She has the money and he has the title, so they'll both be titled and stinking rich by the end of the ceremony."

A sneaky grin crossed her face. "And so will we! She told me on the phone she's looking at $200 a head. I mean, obviously we'll have to buy the ingredients, outsource a lot of cooking and hire a wait staff of a million, but still, that's a lot of money."

"Yes, it is. We could still probably each take home at least $50,000, if not more," DeeDee said. "Wow, Susie. You weren't kidding about taking our business to the next level. Where did you find her?"

"Oh, this Seattle high-life forum where I've been doing some networking, you know, it's a form of marketing."

"Amazing," DeeDee said. "What can I say but well done? So how do you want us to proceed with this?"

"I've put together three potential menus," Susie said. "One traditional, one with a twist, and one totally out there, like what we did with Tobias. I tried to incorporate some English dishes as well to appeal to that side of the family." She took the menus out of her large tote bag and laid them out on the table. They were printed on a thick cream card stock and had little design flourishes.

"These look great! You've done a beautiful job, Susie."

"I should have checked with you before I printed them to see if they were okay with you, but I was up all night doing them, and I knew you were resting up, so I didn't want to bother you."

"Thank you," DeeDee said. "But next time, feel free to interrupt me." She looked over the menus and thought Susie's dish selections were excellent. "These look fantastic, Susie. I'm feeling very confident about going to the meeting with them."

Susie breathed a sigh of relief. "Oh, thank goodness. I was worried you wouldn't like them."

DeeDee laughed. "You worry too much."

"You're probably right," Susie said, putting the menus back in her bag. "I mean, I called a meeting before the meeting, which is probably only going to exacerbate my nerves." She looked at her watch. "We need to get to the ferry, so we can get there on time."

"We'll be there in plenty of time, probably a little early. You know what I'd like to do?"

"I'd like to call Tanya and see if she has a couple of minutes to talk to us. It's right on our way, and I'd like to ask her about the women who left the dinner for a while at Tobias'."

"That would be fine. I was afraid you wanted to bring her to the meeting with our potential client, and I didn't think that would be such a good idea." She was quiet for a moment and then said, "Actually, that will take my mind off my nerves. I'll give her a call now."

Tanya was a university student. She only did waitressing as a side job. When DeeDee called her, she told her she was studying in the library and would be happy to come out and talk to her.

When they got off the ferry, they drove to the university campus and nearly got lost following the confusing signage.

"How does anyone find their way around here?" DeeDee wondered. But they finally found the front of the library and saw Tanya sitting on a bench under a tree, waiting for them. They hurried over to her.

"Hi, Tanya," DeeDee said. "Sorry to drag you away from your studies like this."

Tanya flashed them a grin. "I don't mind, seriously. I'm studying Engineering, and it gets so technical sometimes my brain freezes up. It's like a computer when it jams, and it won't do anything. Then you have to restart it. When that happens, I usually have to go for a walk or something, so I was glad for the interruption."

Susie nodded. "Consider us as your reset."

They sat down beside her on the bench.

"Remember the night that Angel Bridges was murdered and we were talking about the people you'd seen leave the room?" DeeDee asked. "I'd like to show you some photographs of people involved with the opera, and see if you recognize any of the women."

"Sure," Tanya said. "Actually, I did this already with Detective Kirton."

"Oh?" DeeDee said. "Did you find it easy to remember?" She rummaged in her purse to get her phone out. She hadn't brought along the program, but she could look the players up online.

"Yes, once I saw the faces, I knew instantly who I'd seen," Tanya said. "Luckily I have quite a good memory for faces. I hope it will help with the investigation."

"I'm sure it will," Susie said kindly.

DeeDee was still on her phone, looking up Lola Newman and Siobhan Whitehead. "I don't mean to be rude," Tanya said. "But why are you asking me? Don't get me wrong, I'm very happy to tell you. I'll tell anyone who asks, because I know what I saw. It's not a secret or anything. But I'm just curious."

DeeDee wasn't sure about telling her that Tobias Crank had asked Jake's private investigation firm to take on the case. She was concerned that Tanya could decide to go back to the police with that information, which might further antagonize Detective Kirton. But she couldn't think of what else to say.

Luckily, Susie came to the rescue. "Detective Kirton said that DeeDee or I could have been the one who murdered Angel, since we had access to the kitchen, and we could have poisoned the champagne."

Tanya gasped. "No!"

"Unfortunately, yes," Susie said. "We're trying to figure out who might have done it, so we can present the evidence to the police, and make sure we're not falsely accused."

"I'm so sorry that's happening," Tanya said. "That's horrible. It must be terribly stressful."

"Don't worry about us," DeeDee said. "I'm sure he's not really serious about it. We're probably being overly cautious."

"Better safe than sorry, though," Susie added.

"Here you go," DeeDee said, showing Tanya the phone. She started by showing her the older woman who played Queen Tiye, Siobhan Whitehead. "What about her?"

"Yes, she definitely left the room."

"Are you 100% certain?" DeeDee asked.

"Yes, because I remember admiring her dress. It was really lovely, sort of art deco, flapper-girl era style."

"Okay," DeeDee said. She googled Lola Newman, since there was no picture of her on the official site of the opera, and quickly found her picture. "What about her?"

"No, she didn't go out," Tanya said. "I remember, because she was flirting with everyone in sight and laughing very loudly. She flirted with the British guy…"

"Laurence Powers," Susie said.

"And then when he left the room to go to the bathroom, she flirted with the guy on the other side of her. Then when Laurence came back in, she switched back over to him again. Yes, I clearly remember her."

"Thanks, Tanya," DeeDee said. "What about these ladies?" There were pictures of six women on the opera website with the caption, *Daughters of Akhnaten: Beketate, Meretaten, Maketaten, Ankhesenpaaten,*

Neferneferuaten, and Sotopenre.

Tanya looked at each face for a moment before she said, "I'm not really sure, to be honest. Sorry. Detective Kirton didn't show me that photo."

Susie and DeeDee looked at each other, eyebrows raised.

"Okay, thanks so much, Tanya," DeeDee said. "We really appreciate it."

"You're welcome," Tanya said. "By the way, please let me know if you have any more waitressing work."

"We sure will," Susie said. "You were very professional and easy to work with last time."

Tanya gave them a genuine smile as she got up. "Thanks. And thanks for being my 'reset.' I feel ready to get back in there and study."

DeeDee smiled. "Great. See you, Tanya."

As they walked back to the parking lot, DeeDee said, "I really thought Lola Newman could have had something to do with it. But she didn't leave the table at dinner, and she seemed to have reacted normally to Angel Bridges' death. I think we may have to look elsewhere."

"What about Siobhan Whitehead, then?" Susie said. "Tanya said she left the table. Do we know anything about her?"

"Nothing," DeeDee said. "She was really kind to me at the dinner party. That's all I know."

"Her kindness could be a front for her evil, murderous ways," Susie said.

DeeDee laughed in spite of herself. "That sounded so dramatic,

Susie. I think you've been around the opera set for too long."

Susie chuckled. "Actually, I liked them. Anyway, a flair for the dramatic never hurt anyone."

"I disagree, since in this case, it murdered someone," DeeDee said. "I think you're right, though, the next port of call should be Siobhan Whitehead. I want to find out more about her."

CHAPTER THIRTEEN

It turned out they didn't get the job. The lady they met was very condescending and snooty. She outright asked DeeDee what brand her bag was. When DeeDee said, "Fendi," the woman laughed and said, "Oh, yes, I remember, from 2011. Don't you think it's time to update it?"

That was when they'd walked in the door, and the conversation went downhill from there. She tore apart every single item on every single one of the three sample menus, which was even more annoying because it made the meeting take a long time, particularly when it looked like it wasn't going to go anywhere anyway.

She seemed to take pleasure in humiliating them by asking unnecessary questions and making difficult demands. DeeDee kept a smile on her face, but countered everything she said in her mind.

"Who serves smoked salmon at a wedding?" the woman asked.

A lot of people actually, DeeDee thought, *but you probably don't know because you're so unpleasant nobody would invite you to their wedding.*

"You're thinking of serving lobster? That is so déclassé."

As are your bad manners, DeeDee countered in her mind.

"An English trifle?" she asked with a tinkly little laugh. "We're not at a picnic in the park!"

I wish I was right now. In fact, I wish I was anywhere else but here, so I wouldn't have to listen to your voice.

Eventually, when they were halfway through the third menu, the most exotic one, which was excellent ammunition for the woman's contempt, DeeDee said, "It seems you don't like any of the ideas we've come up with. Did you want to work on putting some new ideas together, with our assistance? Or perhaps we're not the right fit for this event?"

Susie shot her a look, but DeeDee had no intention of sucking up to this rude woman, not even for $50,000. Her dignity was worth more. Besides, if they were going to work together, she needed to establish some boundaries and show they weren't to be pushed around or belittled.

The woman abruptly stood up. "I think it's time for you to leave." She led them through the hallway out the front door and then shut it behind them. Once they were in the car, the windows up, Susie said, "DeeDee! Maybe if we'd just taken all her trash talk, she'd have hired us at the end of it."

"And would you really have wanted to take on a job like that?" DeeDee said, putting the car into gear. "She'd be asking us to serve up our own eyeballs as an appetizer, because her guests are soooo important."

Susie shook her head. "I don't know." She sounded quite annoyed.

"I know you worked hard on it," DeeDee said. "But she isn't the only client out there in the world. There are tons more. They just need to know who we are and what we do. Maybe we should do the exotic angle, like you suggested. Maybe we could get a feature piece in a magazine?"

Susie started to perk up. "That's a good idea."

"We could cater a special party, just for them, and have them taste some weird and wonderful creations to report back on favorably. Of course, doing something like that could get quite expensive."

"I think it's worth it," Susie said. "You're right. Forget you, old grouchy Mrs. Winterbottom."

"Anyway, you didn't even check Red Flag Number One," DeeDee said. "It's her daughter's wedding, yet she's organizing everything. Doesn't that say 'control freak' to you?"

Susie shrugged. "Maybe. She told me her daughter's too lazy to organize anything."

DeeDee chuckled. "Well, that might be true. Who knows? Lovely family. Anyways, the point is, we'll get better jobs. Trust me."

DeeDee felt quite buoyant and confident about it, but when she got home after dropping Susie off at the café to pick up her car, her mood flattened out a little. It was late fall and she noticed over the years, that sometimes her mood got colder as the weather did, kind of a personal change of seasons. She tried to ignore it, but she was beginning to get depressed.

Jake was at the office with Al, working on their big case. He'd already told her he'd be working late. She wandered around the house, unable to commit to anything taking any effort and ate junk food, which was quite unlike her. It was raining and gray outside which didn't help any.

As she lay on her bed looking out the window, Balto and Yukon jumped up and laid down next to her. Balto put his paw on her arm and looked at her, worried.

She smiled for the first time that afternoon. "Is this an intervention?" she asked with a chuckle. And it was. Feeling warm inside, she hugged both of the big husky dogs. "I love you guys. Just ignore me. I think the shock of the murder is catching up with me, plus I can't figure out why Jake didn't tell me about the mysterious death connected to his case.

"Then there's the fact that Detective Kirton more or less accused me of murdering Angel. And the stress of not knowing who did it. And losing the contract today. They're not all big things, but they add up, and now I'm feeling kind of sorry for myself. Don't worry. I'll be fine in a couple of hours."

DeeDee still hadn't talked to Jake about him withholding the information from her. She hadn't decided how to broach the subject with him, so she'd put it in the back of her mind. Now she was ready to talk about it, but she couldn't call him at his office and ask him, so it wasn't going to happen.

She sighed deeply, and decided to get out of bed.

"Even though I have to take the ferry again, think I'll go talk to Tobias Crank," she said to the dogs. "I've got to do something other than lie here and feel sorry for myself."

*****

"Look," DeeDee said to Tobias Crank. She'd gone to visit him at his apartment to find out anything she could, and in spite of herself, all her frustration was coming out. "I know you had an argument with Angel Bridges, and you need to tell me about it, because I'm sure someone else must have heard it other than me. It makes you look suspicious."

Tobias became pale. "I don't know if anyone else heard it. I didn't even know that you'd heard it."

"Well, I did. And honestly, Tobias, it makes you look pretty bad."

"Yes, okay, you're right. I do have a motive," he said. "Angel wasn't an opera player. She had the voice, and she had the star quality, but she's a movie actress. It's different. She didn't want to follow my direction. She had all of the subtle looks and gestures that work really well on a big screen, but they can't be seen in an opera. She wouldn't listen to me. I'll admit I wanted her out of the contract, and she refused, but that was no reason for me to kill her. What kind of insane person would do that?"

DeeDee flopped down on one of the Louis XIV chairs and sighed. "I agree with you, Tobias, but unfortunately there are a lot of insane people out there. How are people going to know you're not one of them? You have to admit that's a pretty strong motive."

"But I'm not the only one with the motive," Tobias shot back. "What about Laurence Powers? They were always arguing. And don't forget about Lola Newman. She could have done it to get the lead role. Although if she was the one who murdered Angel, it didn't work out very well for her, since I'm recasting the lead and she's going to remain as the cover. She's only covering until it's cast. I suppose if the new lead drops dead, then we'll have our answer. Lola will be the one," he said with a chuckle.

"That's really not funny," DeeDee responded with a pained look on her face.

"A black sense of humor for some light relief, is all," Tobias said.

"Hmm."

"I think you should also look into Angel's husband," Tobias said.

DeeDee frowned. "What about him? He couldn't have committed the murder. He wasn't even in town."

"True, but he could have sent someone to do it."

"Tobias, you knew all your guests personally, didn't you?"

"No, not all of them," he said. "There were five or six who were recommended by the Opera House, so I just added them to my list without questioning them. One of them could have been planted by

Angel's husband."

"But why?" DeeDee said. "Why would he want to do that?"

"Why would any husband want to kill his wife? But they do. All the time. Especially types like him."

"What kind of type is he?"

"The jealous type."

"Ah," DeeDee said. "Yes."

"He didn't like her being away from home," Tobias explained. "She didn't confide in me or anything, but a few times I heard her begging him to understand she wasn't cheating on him. Sometimes she was even crying."

"Well, I have to agree. That sounds pretty bad," DeeDee said.

"Yes, and it was as if he was 'around,' without even being here, because she carried so much of his spirit with her. Everything that happened, she had to make a comment on it that somehow related back to him."

"Like…?"

"Oh, I don't know… Let's say, someone gave me a bottle of wine. She might then say, 'That's one of Julius' favorites, but his real favorite is Chateau Lafite Rothschild. He said he would collect them, only, he likes drinking them too much, so his collection is back to zero before it's even started.'"

He sighed heavily. "That sort of thing. That endless commentary that lets you know that either one, she's still in the first flush of love and hasn't the self-awareness to stop talking about him, or two, he's convinced her he's the most important person in the world, much more important than she is, and everything he does, says, thinks or feels is absolutely fascinating and of utmost significance. I sensed it was the latter."

"Hmm," DeeDee said, as she stood up and started pacing around the room. "Well, a man with that kind of character sounds like he has a very fragile sense of self, and is trying to bolster it with, well, her, really. I wonder if it helps his ego, the fact that she's a movie star, or hurts it, because she's more successful than him."

"Both, probably," Tobias replied.

"When I met him, he seemed like a very nice man," DeeDee said. "But I know about these manipulative types. My friend had a husband like that, a total narcissist. He was absolutely lovely and charming to everyone outside the home, but he was a monster once the doors to their home were closed.

"None of us had any idea that he'd been hitting her and saying cruel things to her for years and years. We thought they were the closest couple we knew, so I can see how Julius could have appeared kind, but actually been something entirely different."

"Yes."

DeeDee continued to pace, thinking deeply. "Do you really think he could have sent someone to the party through the opera house to poison Angel? Honestly, Tobias, it sounds a little far-fetched to me. Don't these types usually snap during a jealous rage and strangle their wives, or get a gun or something?"

"I don't know," Tobias said. "But if he's the smooth, cool and calculating type, maybe he didn't have to snap at all. Maybe he planned it as calmly as someone else might plan what they're having for dinner that night."

A shiver went down DeeDee's spine. How could someone ever do that to their spouse, the person they were supposed to love and want the best for?

"I suppose he could have..." DeeDee said. "Maybe the motive

was a mix of jealousy and money. He must be receiving huge amounts of money right now. Millions and millions. But if he had such firm control over her, he wouldn't need to kill her to get access to all her money. He'd already have it. Hmm…"

"Maybe it was just jealousy," Tobias said. "Jealous because she's doing so well in her career. Jealous because she's away from home working closely with other men, where he can't watch her and control her."

"It really could be that," DeeDee said. Her phone beeped, so she took it out of her pocket and saw that it was Susie calling. She said goodbye to Tobias and left his apartment, deciding to call Susie later.

The whole way down in the elevator, her brain buzzed with the idea of Julius being the killer. Did it make sense? Was it crazy? She couldn't tell. The first rush of the idea was always amazing. But it had to settle down into normality so she could pick the idea apart, look for flaws and inconsistencies. It was no good to run with the idea before she'd taken time to really analyze it.

Plus, the irony of the situation was not lost on her – Tobias, another suspect, being the one to bring this theory to her. Maybe he was bringing it up to throw her off the trail. To steer her in another direction, away from his own guilt.

Or then again, maybe he was just trying to help.

It was so hard to tell. Impossible, even.

To put it mildly, it had not been a good day. And she still had to talk to Jake about his lying by omission. "I think tonight calls for a large tub of ice cream," she said to herself, and once she'd left the ferry, she went to the store to get one – cinnamon and caramel with oat clusters – before heading home.

CHAPTER FOURTEEN

The evening didn't get better. It got worse.

DeeDee didn't feel much like talking to Jake, who sensed it and left her alone, concentrating on his paperwork. She soaked in a bubble bath for far longer than was necessary, with her ice cream and some white wine. She'd just changed into her comfort pajamas when she heard a car pulling up in front of the house, and she saw the flash of headlights.

"Oh dear," she groaned, going to the bedroom door. "Who is that?"

It turned out to be Cassie and Al. It seemed the situation between them had escalated.

DeeDee got downstairs just as Jake was opening the door for them, Yukon and Balto right behind her.

Cassie entered the house like a human whirlwind. She looked very upset and angry. "Okay," she said. "I've had it. I want to know what's going on in your investigation, and I want to know it now. Jake, Al said the two of you agreed to keep DeeDee in the dark, but that doesn't work for me. DeeDee and I need to know what the two of you are getting us into. Are we in danger?"

Jake sighed and looked at DeeDee, who was standing in the doorway to the kitchen and living area, leaning against the doorjamb.

"She's right, Jake," DeeDee said. "I found out you hid the fact a potential whistleblower got offed by someone who had something to do with that company. It might be the same guys you're investigating. We need to know the truth."

Jake and Al looked at each other. Al was uncharacteristically quiet. He shrugged. "Looks like we ain't got no choice, Jake."

"You got that right," Cassie said.

"Let's go into the great room," DeeDee said.

Once they were all sitting down, Cassie said, "So?" as she leaned forward, her elbows on her knees. She meant business, and everyone knew it. She was normally such a calm, placid person that seeing her like this had everyone rattled.

Jake sighed. "All right. Yes, there was a potential whistleblower who got killed. But listen, here's the thing. We took the evidence to the DA, and they told us we were not to speak about the case to anyone. They're preparing to charge Joshua Jessup with murder."

Cassie sighed with relief. "Oh, thank goodness. I thought you two were going to do something stupid. Get guns and take your chances or something crazy."

"C'mon, Cassie!" Al said. "After my days in the mob, ya' think I'd do somethin' that dumb?"

"Sorry, babe," Cassie said. She smiled, and sat back. "What a relief."

"You're not to say a word to anyone, all right?" Jake asked. "Either of you. We shouldn't even be telling you this."

"But wasn't it in our wedding vows?" Cassie said. You know, 'Tell your wife everything?' Well, okay, I know it's not, but telling us sure would have prevented a lot of stress for everybody. Don't you want our support? You men think you have to soldier on and deal with everything on your own."

"Right!" DeeDee said. "Wait, what have you actually been doing all this time? When did this happen?"

"A week ago," Al said. "We been lookin' at new cases."

"Including yours," Jake said. "Laurence Powers is someone you need to look into. I was going to tell you about him tomorrow. I found out tonight that he was arrested for domestic violence in his first marriage. He's married to someone else now and has a few drunk and disorderly and domestic violence charges stemming from his relationship with her. I'm thinking, what if he was in a relationship with Angel Bridges, a secret relationship? And he killed her."

DeeDee swallowed. "I guess it's a possibility." She paused. "I think I'll go see him tomorrow."

"I'd like to go with you," Jake said. "For all his suave English ways, he seems like a dangerous man. But I can't do it tomorrow. I'm meeting with a client on a new case. And don't worry, it's a woman who wants to confirm that her husband is cheating on her. No murders involved."

"Ima thinkin' I'll go with ya', DeeDee," Al said. "I'll jes' switch back to my Mafia man bravado if'n he gives so much as a hint he's gonna' turn nasty."

"Thanks, Al," DeeDee said.

*****

The next day DeeDee and Al took her car and went to visit Laurence in his suite at one of the most expensive hotels in Seattle. This time, they had an in. Laurence and Tobias got along very well, and Tobias asked him to see DeeDee as a favor.

It was very clear Laurence was doing Tobias a favor, and he wasn't very gracious about it.

He didn't offer them a drink when he invited them into his exclusive suite. He didn't say much at all, just, "Oh, hello." Then he turned around and walked down the hallway and into another room. DeeDee and Al followed him without being invited.

It turned out he was working on a painting, and he immediately resumed working on it when he returned to the room. He was by the window, and had laid a bedsheet out underneath his easel. He dabbed away at his painting of the Seattle skyline. DeeDee thought it was actually quite good.

She and Al gave each other a look indicating they both felt he was being rude. But DeeDee felt he was the kind of person who'd be eating out of her hand with enough compliments.

"That's an exquisite painting," she said, walking toward it.

"No one told me you'd be bringing one of your henchmen with you," he said. "Is this an arranged hit?"

"Don't be silly," DeeDee said. "This is Al. He's married to my dear friend, Cassie."

"You're blocking my light," Laurence said tersely.

DeeDee moved back.

"So, Al," Laurence said. "Do you talk, or are you all brawn and have so few brains you can't formulate a sentence?"

DeeDee turned and looked wide-eyed at Al, having a hard time believing how rude Laurence was being.

To DeeDee's surprise, Al laughed. "Laurie my man, you jes' don't got no manners, do ya'?"

"I don't need to have manners," Laurence said. "Manners are for the aspirational. Those who have something they need to prove, licking other people's boots for approval and favors."

"New one on me," Al said. "Don't s'pose ya' got many friends with yer' 'tude, hey, Laurie?"

"My name is Laurence," he said, not looking away from his painting.

"Awright, Laurence it is," Al said. "I jes'…"

"What are you two really doing here?" Laurence asked as he continued to paint.

"Were you in a romantic relationship with Angel Bridges?" DeeDee blurted out, surprising even herself.

That made Laurence turn around and look at her, but only briefly. By the time he replied, he'd turned back to his painting. "Don't be preposterous."

Al decided to go along with DeeDee's line of questioning. "Yeah, ya' probly' were," he said. "Can't blame ya', neither. Beautiful woman, she was, but she wouldn't leave her husband. Or maybe she was flirtin' with Tobias. It jes' got to be too much for ya', didn't it?"

Laurence's voice was even. "If you're insinuating I killed her, you are tragically mistaken."

"The arguing behind the scenes was a cover, wasn't it?" DeeDee said. "A cover for your illicit love affair."

"I should have the two of you committed to a mental hospital," Laurence said, his voice icy cool.

"Fine," DeeDee said. "So you weren't having an affair with her.

But the fact remains the two of you were always arguing. Everyone can attest to that. So that's the reason you killed her. Because you hated her, and felt she was a mere movie star in comparison with your Shakespearean greatness. She was getting more attention than you were and you didn't like it. Let's face it, she stole the show."

"I assure you I do not have that fragile of an ego," Laurence said. "For you to even be able to make up such a story indicates you have issues yourself. Perhaps a qualified psychotherapist could help you."

"Throw all the insults ya' want," Al said. "Nothin' I ain't heard before. And DeeDee ain't no delicate flower, either. We ain't gonna' be put off askin' ya' questions jes' because yer' flingin' insults at us."

Laurence put down his brush and looked at them. "Who are you two? The gestapo? What on earth is this? I know you're not with the police," he said, looking at DeeDee. "You're a mere caterer."

"A mere caterer," Al said, rolling his eyes and laughing. "Get a loada' this guy, DeeDee. Reckon the dude thinks he owns the world and everythin' that walks on it."

DeeDee was glad Al stood up for her, as the 'mere caterer' comment did hurt just a tiny bit.

"Fine," she said. "Well, if you're not the killer, you must have some thoughts about who the murderer could be. What about Siobhan Whitehead?"

"She'd never do such a thing," Laurence said.

"Lola Newman?" DeeDee said.

Laurence's face crinkled impatiently. "Who?"

"Angel Bridges' cover. She only plays Nefertiti opposite you now," DeeDee said.

"Oh, the blonde bimbo. Well, I guess she could have done it, if she was completely deranged, to get the part of Nefertiti. But psychopaths like that are few and far between," he said. "I still have no idea why you've assumed the roles of Holmes and Watson, but since you have, I would suggest you look at more feasible explanations. A lover or husband, for example."

"That's why we came here in the first place," DeeDee said. "Or do you have a very short memory? We were wondering if you were the lover who killed her."

"I'm very happily married, thank you," he said. "Now, get out of my hotel suite or I'll call the police and let them know what you're up to. I'm sure it can't be legal. I have a busy day ahead of me and don't have time for such nonsense. Good day."

CHAPTER FIFTEEN

"That certainly went well," Al said as they walked out of Laurence's hotel.

"Tell me," DeeDee said. "Any gut feelings?"

"Nope." Al thrust his hands deep into his pockets. "Ima tellin' ya' I learned in the mob not to go by 'em, even if I do. Too often, it's the guy ya' least expect."

"That's true enough," DeeDee said.

"Love to stick 'round, DeeDee," Al said. "But I'm on the hunt fer clients. We gotta' set up a website an' do all this crazy stuff they call 'digital marketin'. My head's explodin' with it. Gonna' hire someone to help, but I still gotta' know what I'm talkin' 'bout, and thanks to that annoyin' husband of yers', somehow it ends up bein' my job." He grinned. "Give him a good smack over the head for me when ya' get home, will ya'?"

DeeDee laughed. "Perhaps a light tap."

Al shook his head at her with a disappointed smile. "Yer' lettin' the team down, DeeDee."

DeeDee made a face at him. "Anyway, I'm not going home. I

think I'm going to see if Siobhan Whitehead is at the apartment she's renting. I still haven't talked to her."

"Which one's that again?"

"Oh, come on, Al. You're supposed to know the ins and outs of this. She's the lady who played Queen Tiye, in the opera."

Al grinned. "Which one's that again?"

"Ugh!" DeeDee said. "I won't waste any more time on you. Okay if you take a cab to the ferry when you finish up here in town?"

"Sure," Al said.

"Say hi to Cassie for me."

"Will do," he said as he headed down the street.

DeeDee looked around for somewhere she could buy a sandwich or burrito. She didn't want a big lunch, just something to keep her going. She found a little deli and ordered what turned out to be a very 'artisan' sandwich.

She thought she was getting a simple ham and cheese, but it turned out to be parma ham, tomato, onions, lettuce, avocado, and Swiss cheese, and was absolutely delicious, though incredibly expensive.

DeeDee decided to leave her car in the parking garage, so she hailed a cab and took off towards Siobhan Whitehead's apartment, not wanting to fight parking again in downtown Seattle. After she entered the high-rise building, she spoke to the concierge. "I'm afraid she's out at the moment," the concierge said.

"Thanks," DeeDee said. She took out her cell and called Tobias, to see if he'd know where Siobhan was, but the call went to voicemail. She sighed. "All right, I'll come back another time."

Stepping out onto the cold street, she wondered what she should do next. It didn't seem like she was getting anywhere with the investigation, and she was feeling frustrated.

The only option was to go home. Then a thought occurred to her. Maybe she should go to the opera house and see if there was anyone of interest there. Maybe they were in rehearsal, or maybe there was a matinee, although Laurence hadn't looked like he was going anywhere soon. She looked at the website on her phone and saw that no matinee was scheduled for that day. But maybe there was a rehearsal.

It turned out she was right.

But it was no ordinary rehearsal.

Because Tobias Crank had gone AWOL.

She managed to talk her way into the theater, telling the guard that she was "Tobias Crank's culinary manager" and had to "see him urgently." Siobhan Whitehead and Lola Newman were on stage in their regular clothes, rather than the heavy grandeur of the Egyptian costumes.

But the person yelling directions at them wasn't Tobias Crank. It was a very slim woman, perhaps in her 50s, with a short dark haircut and a severe manner. The way she was yelling at them was quite formidable. She sounded short-tempered and looked very unapproachable.

But DeeDee was no wallflower. She made her way down the aisle, and walked right up to her.

"Yes?" the woman said impatiently.

DeeDee's eyes quickly scanned the stage, and again she felt that she needed to talk to Siobhan Whitehead at some point, and soon. But there was a mounting anxiety buzzing through her, and she had another question. "Do you know where Tobias Crank is?" she asked.

"No, I don't," she said. "Which is why I'm here." She rolled her eyes. "He probably had a wild party last night and is sleeping. It's not unheard of for him. Anyway…" She looked DeeDee up and down, and not at all approvingly. "Who's asking?"

"I catered the party for him the night Angel Bridges was murdered, and we've been talking about things. I wasn't able to get through to his cell, so I decided to see if he was here. Maybe I should go to his apartment…?"

"Don't bother," the woman said. "I sent a stagehand over there in a cab earlier. He's not there, or more likely, not answering the door. Now, I really have to get back to this."

"But do you think that the person who killed Angel Bridges could have…"

"Killed him?" The woman said with a laugh. "There's no need to be overdramatic. I'm sure he'll turn up in a few hours."

"I think I should notify the police." As much as DeeDee didn't want to talk to Detective Kirton, she was becoming increasingly worried.

"Your call," the woman said impatiently. "Bye, then."

"Just one more thing," DeeDee said. "Do you know what time you'll be finished with the rehearsal? I want to speak to Siobhan Whitehead about something."

"She'll be done in a half hour, so you can wait. Sit down somewhere and don't talk to me, please. You're interrupting my flow."

"Sorry," DeeDee said. "And thanks."

DeeDee took a seat a short distance away from the woman and watched the rehearsal continue. Both Lola Newman and Siobhan Whitehead looked at DeeDee as she went to her seat, and she couldn't help but notice that they looked a little worried.

They continued with their scene, and DeeDee was left to wonder why they looked worried? Were they just as concerned about Tobias Crank, as she was? Or was it something deeper?

With nothing else to focus on, her mind began to wander into crazy possibilities. Maybe they hatched the murder plot together. Lola Newman didn't leave the room at dinner, but Siobhan Whitehead did. Maybe she was the one who delivered the poisoned drink to Angel, while Lola was the mastermind. But why? What would the motive be?

With Angel Bridges out of the way, they would be the two leading ladies of the production. But why would Siobhan Whitehead care about that? She already had her part. She didn't need to help Lola. So why would she? Maybe she was jealous of all the attention Angel Bridges was getting. Or maybe there was something much deeper going on. Thoughts were tangling themselves up in DeeDee's head until she felt utterly confused.

But it didn't take long for the director woman to say, "All right, we're done. Nice job. Siobhan, this lady wants to speak to you. I'd like you to do that immediately, please. I don't want her hanging around all afternoon."

Siobhan looked a little shocked, and shared a look with Lola, but then she came down the steps at the side of the stage and walked towards DeeDee, who had stood up out of respect.

When Siobhan came over, she said, "Sit down, sit down, please, DeeDee."

DeeDee was surprised. "You remember me, then?"

"Of course," Siobhan said with a smile, sitting down herself. "How could anyone forget your wonderful cooking?" She sighed. "And the tragic night that lay ahead, unbeknownst to all of us."

"Yes," DeeDee said, immediately at ease. There was something about Siobhan that just made her feel comfortable. She made a conscious decision not to be lulled into a false sense of security, but it wasn't that easy. Siobhan felt like an instant kindred friend. She sat up straighter and tried not to smile. "I'm worried about Tobias Crank."

"So am I," Siobhan said.

"I called him, but it went right to voicemail," DeeDee said. "I'm trying not to let my imagination run wild, but I can't help but wonder if…"

"If he's in danger?" Siobhan Whitehead said.

"Yes. After all, the police haven't caught the murderer yet. Whoever murdered Angel is still on the loose."

"I know," Siobhan said. She shuddered. "I keep telling myself it's unlikely anything has happened to him, though. Because then we'd have something like a serial killer on our hands, and that's very rare. I'd say it's more likely he's become depressed and is staying in bed eating ice cream, not answering the phone or the door."

"Do you think?" DeeDee said. "I got the impression that he'd move heaven and earth to be at every rehearsal and performance. He seems most grateful to his benefactor, Lowell Marks. I don't think he'd want to let him down."

Siobhan sighed. "Trust me, all that goes out of one's head when someone's in the grip of serious depression." It sounded like she spoke from experience, but DeeDee didn't want to pry.

"Let me level with you," DeeDee said. "Tobias asked me to investigate the murder. One of my wait staff said you were one of the people who left the dining room during dinner."

"I went to the bathroom."

"Can anyone verify that?"

"Unfortunately not," she said. "But I didn't kill Angel Bridges, I really didn't. I realize that you don't know me very well, but if you did, you'd know the idea is preposterous. I'm not that kind of person."

DeeDee nodded, wanting to say, 'that's what all murderers say,' but she didn't. "Do you have any history with Angel Bridges?"

"None," Siobhan said. "I'd never even met her until we began rehearsals a couple of months ago."

"Did the two of you get along?"

"I tend not to bring too many emotions with me to work," she said. "I just keep it professional, so there was no reason for the two of us not to get along. She was professional with me, too. We weren't best friends, by any means, in fact we never spoke on a personal level. But there was no animosity either. It was just a neutral relationship."

"Okay," DeeDee said. "Do you know why anyone would have wanted to kill her? Can you think of any motives?"

"I really didn't know her well enough to say," Siobhan said. "I know there was some drama between cast members, and Tobias as well, but I kept completely out of it. I've been in opera a long time, and the one thing I've learned is to avoid drama at all costs. I just stick to the drama on the stage. The only people I'd say I'm particularly close with are Lola Newman, the covering for Nefertiti, who I was just on stage with, and Tobias."

DeeDee smiled. "All right." *Close to Lola, huh? Did that mean anything?* DeeDee wondered. "Is this the first time you've worked with Lola?"

"Yes," Siobhan said. "But she's very talented. And a very sweet girl. Just a little insecure. She reminds me of…" Her eyes went all faraway, and filled with tears. Then she cleared her throat. "She reminds me of me... when I was young, so I'm trying to share with her what I know."

DeeDee nodded. "That's kind of you."

"Actually, I thought it was rather selfish," Siobhan said. "She didn't ask for all this nurturing and mentoring. I may well be doing it for my own reasons. I'm not sure, but I am sure I'll probably be talking about my motivations in therapy soon," she said with a laugh.

DeeDee laughed along with her. "Well, whatever the case, I'm sure she appreciates the help." She got up from her seat. "I'd better be going. Just one more thing. I'd like to ask you a favor."

"Shoot."

DeeDee handed her a Deelish business card. "If you do manage to get in touch with Tobias, would you please let me know? I'm going to be worried sick if I don't hear from him by the end of the day."

"Certainly," Siobhan said with a smile. "Take care."

As DeeDee was walking out of the theater, she felt warm and safe. Such was the effect Siobhan Whitehead had on her. It was so hard not to believe her. So hard to question what she said. So hard to believe she could be lying.

When DeeDee got out of the opera house, she tried to call Tobias, but again it went to his voicemail. She headed back to the parking garage, trying not to worry too much, and left for the ferry to take her home to Bainbridge Island.

When DeeDee got home, Jake was buzzing with nervous energy. He'd obviously been waiting for her to come home, since the moment she stepped in the front door, he started talking in rapid fire, without pausing to let her reply, or even take a breath.

"Hey, babe. Guess what? The DA approached us again. They want us to continue with the meeting at Canlis, and they're gonna' send an FBI agent along with Al to try and wiggle something out of Joshua Jessup. They're hoping to get something on that very same night and arrest him. They have a body of evidence, but they just want something final."

"Oh dear," DeeDee said. "A joint project with the DA and FBI..."

Jake looked at her worriedly, yet hopefully. "What do you think?"

DeeDee didn't know what to think. It sounded so incredibly dangerous. And at the same time, it also sounded like the biggest move in Jake's career. She stayed silent for a several long moments.

"So?" he said. "I thought you'd have something to say about it."

"Give me a minute," DeeDee said. She went over to coffee maker and nodded towards it. "I need coffee."

He nodded back, and they looked at each other for what seemed a long time, but in reality, was only a moment. The air was intense, though DeeDee didn't quite know what with. Perhaps his feeling. His intensity.

DeeDee had imagined herself sitting down and sipping her coffee before she answered him, but a gut feeling rushed in, and she knew exactly what to say. "Do it."

Jake couldn't help but burst into a grin. "Really? Are you serious?"

"Yes," DeeDee said. "You look so happy, and we both know this is a huge career move for you."

"It really is," Jake said. "Thank you so much for seeing it that way. I wanted to go for it, but the last thing I want to do is to make you worry about me. And I didn't want to hide anything from you again, considering how that went last time."

DeeDee laughed. "Darn straight. You want a cup of coffee?"

"Sure, that would be nice," he said. He paused. "The thing about this is, honey…"

"Yes?"

"It's tomorrow night, and I want you to come with me."

DeeDee laughed. "Oh, so we have plenty of time to prepare." She surprised herself by taking it so lightly.

"You still willing to do it?" he asked, cringing slightly, knowing it was a big ask.

Maybe the reason she was taking it so lightly was due to her craving some adventure, since she was getting nowhere on the Angel case. "Sure, what the heck. Count me in!" DeeDee said.

CHAPTER SIXTEEN

That evening, DeeDee and Jake passed their time enjoyably. They spoke briefly about the dinner at Canlis the following night, and what they would both wear while Yukon and Balto played together in the hallway.

Jake said, "Honestly, there's nothing to worry about. The only thing is if I have to go over to their headquarters for any reason, which is very, very unlikely, you'd have to get a cab to take you to the ferry. Or, if you don't want to come back to the island, you can go to Al and Cassie's, or even a hotel, if you'd feel safer there. But honestly, I don't think anything will happen, I really don't."

"It's fine," DeeDee said. "So our emergency plan is I go outside and get a cab to either Cassie's or to a hotel, whichever feels safer to me. Got it."

"Great," Jake said. "Thank you so much for supporting me on this. Once this is over, I can dedicate a lot more time to the Angel Bridges case. How's it going so far?"

DeeDee sighed. "Honestly? Not all that great. Al and I talked to Laurence, and that was a total joke. He gave nothing away, I mean nothing. I spoke to Lola, and the only thing of note there was that Angel's husband turned up while I was there.

"Siobhan Whitehead didn't give much away either, other than that she's quite close to Lola and is a mentor of sorts for her. But there's nothing conclusive coming up. At the moment I'm just waiting for Tobias Crank to come back from wherever he is so I can pick his brain. I think I should have zeroed in on him from the beginning. Not because I think he did it, but because he's the opera's director, and he has the most information on everyone."

"Where did he go?"

"No one knows," DeeDee said. "There was a replacement director at the opera house, because they couldn't find him. He didn't show up for this afternoon's rehearsal."

Jake looked alarmed.

"It's only been a day, though," DeeDee said.

"Yes, but under the circumstances…"

"I know," DeeDee said. "Please don't make me feel more worried than I already am. I keep trying to tell myself nothing is going on and he's fine, but to be honest, it's not easy. The replacement director seemed very nonchalant about it, but I'm getting increasingly concerned."

"Why don't you report him as a missing person?" Jake asked.

"I thought about doing that," DeeDee said, "but don't you have to wait until a certain time period has passed?"

"Normally, yes," Jake said. "But given the circumstances, I'm sure they'll understand you reporting it coming in earlier. As a matter of fact, you can just go to the police here on the island and they'll send it over to the Seattle police department."

"You're absolutely right," DeeDee said. "That's what I need to do. I'm going over there now. I'll feel better if I do." She stood up from the couch and grabbed her keys.

"Do you want me to come with you?" Jake asked?

"No, I'll be okay," DeeDee said. "You need to prepare for tomorrow. Oh, would you take my dress, the blue one, out of the garment bag I have for my better clothes, and let it air for me?"

"Sure," Jake said. He got up and kissed her. "See you soon."

When DeeDee got in the car, she cranked up the radio. The station was playing the greatest hits of the 80s, and she was in the mood. Even though it was a short drive, it was enjoyable. She loved seeing the early evening lights of Seattle across the Sound. She had the window down, and the cold wind felt invigorating to her.

By the time she got to the police station, she felt she could run up a mountain. She just hoped that when the Bainbridge Police sent the report it wouldn't go to Detective Kirton. But at least he wouldn't be at the Bainbridge station, so she wouldn't have to worry that she'd be arrested.

When she went inside, a young officer at the desk said, "Good evening, ma'am. How can I help you?"

"Hello, I want to report a missing person in Seattle. He's been gone less than twenty-four hours, but I'm worried about him."

"It's a common misconception that you need to wait 24 hours," the policeman said. "You can report it at any time. We judge it on a case by case basis as to when we should allocate resources. One moment, please." He did some tapping on his computer. "Name?"

"Tobias Crank."

He typed it in, waited a moment, and then he looked up at her. "Tobias Crank?"

"Yes, he's the director of *Akhnaten* at the Seattle Opera House."

"I know," the cop said. "And he's also in the Seattle jail."

"He's in the Seattle jail?" DeeDee said. "Why?"

"He's in custody."

"You're kidding? For what?"

"He was arrested on suspicion of first-degree murder."

"Of Angel Bridges?"

He nodded.

DeeDee gulped. "Can I talk to him?"

The cop spun around on his chair to look at the clock. "Visiting time finished at 6:00 p.m. But since… well… all right. Just five minutes. We use Skype. I'll call."

"Thank you so much."

"You're welcome. Sign in here, please," he said, pushing a visitor's book towards her. DeeDee wrote her name, the time, and signed it.

"Okay, come on then." He came out from behind the desk with a big bunch of keys, and unlocked a heavy metal side door. He then led her through the open door and into a corridor. "The visiting room is where our Skype is," he said, unlocking another metal door. "Wait inside. They're getting Mr. Crank ready in Seattle. He'll be along in a minute."

"Thank you," DeeDee said.

He closed the door to the little room, but thankfully didn't lock it. Otherwise DeeDee would have felt very claustrophobic. It was a tiny room, with only two chairs in it which filled most of the space and a computer screen on a counter. There was a glass panel with a phone on the wall next to it, and another little space on the other side, where she assumed prisoners being held here at the jail sat.

In a couple of moments, Tobias' face filled up the computer screen. He looked haggard. He was wearing an extremely flamboyant suit in an abstract pattern of lime green and yellow and purple shapes. It was tailored impeccably, but all his gold jewelry was gone, presumably to stop any of the others in custody in the jail from taking it from him, and his hair was standing up on end.

"DeeDee," he said, rather cheerfully, when she smiled at him.

"Five minutes and not a second more," she heard the policeman say to Tobias.

"Tobias," DeeDee said. "They've arrested you?"

"Yes," he said, with a huge smile. "But I'm sure justice will prevail in the end. I'm now very pleased with myself, very pleased indeed, for hiring you and your husband to look into the murder. I'm sure that's why you're visiting me via this computer contraption thing, isn't it? To give the police your leads and 'bust me out of here,' as they say."

DeeDee shifted uncomfortably in her chair. How could she look him dead in the eye and tell him she'd found nothing, nothing at all? DeeDee didn't like to lie, but she didn't know what else she could do to spare his feelings. He looked like he might go crazy if she told him the truth.

"We're on the edge of a breakthrough," she said. "I expect to have everything pieced together over the next couple of days. We just want to make sure our case is airtight."

"Oh, that's wonderful!" Tobias said. "I wish I could reach through this computer and give you a grateful embrace. Alas, we are bound by the rules of the material world."

"Indeed," DeeDee agreed, glad being arrested hadn't had an adverse impact on his exuberant eccentricity. "I won't keep you any longer, Tobias. I want to get back and keep working on putting the case together."

"Who did it?" he asked.

"I don't want to say yet," DeeDee freestyled. "Not until we're 100% certain."

He nodded. "Okay, I understand. I'd appreciate if you didn't let any of the cast know I'm here. Some of them may be foolish enough to believe the police are on the right track. Could you tell them I've taken to bed with a dreadful influenza attack, and I don't want any visitors?"

"Of course," DeeDee said. "I'll call Siobhan and let her know. She was worried about you."

"I suppose that awful woman Tamara took over for me in the meanwhile?"

"The slim woman with the black hair?"

"The very same," he said, his face darkening. "I wouldn't be at all surprised if she gave the cops a false tip so they'd have a reason to arrest me."

"Really?"

"No, well, I don't know. Just get me out of here, DeeDee, please! Being treated like a common criminal is very damaging to my soul."

"I'll do my absolute best, Tobias," DeeDee said, standing up. "I promise."

"Thank you," he said. "I am most indebted." He stood up also and made a little bow.

When DeeDee got home, she didn't feel remotely like continuing the cozy evening she and Jake had been enjoying before she'd left.

"Jake!" she called as she came in the front door. "I need your help!"

He came out of the bedroom with a towel wrapped around him, his hair still wet from a shower. "What happened?"

"Tobias Crank got arrested," she said. "I lied to him and told him we'd nearly wrapped up the case and would get him out of jail sooner rather than later, but the truth is I have no idea who could have killed Angel Bridges. I think it's time to get out our laptops and do some research. Let's see if we can find some dirt on any of these people."

"I'm on it," Jake said, throwing on his jeans and a shirt. He and DeeDee hurried over to the kitchen table, fired up their laptops. and got to work.

"I'll take Laurence Powers and Siobhan Whitehead," DeeDee said. "You take Tobias Crank and Lola Newman. I don't believe Tobias did it, but let's see what we can find out anyway."

Jake interlocked his fingers together, then stretched them out in front of him until they cracked. Then he cracked his neck from side to side. "Okay, now I'm ready. Let's do this. Time to dig up some dirt."

CHAPTER SEVENTEEN

Jake and DeeDee stayed up until the early hours of the morning, doing their best to dig up dirt on their respective suspects. Although they discovered a lot of interesting things about each of them, it wasn't until 2:00 a.m. that they made the discovery that changed everything.

They both gasped out loud.

"I think we've cracked it," Jake whispered.

"I think we have," DeeDee said, her eyes scanning over the information again and again.

They'd put two pieces of information together from two sources. These pieces of information both seemed totally harmless when taken alone, but when put together? They formed a powerful motive. A devastatingly powerful motive.

"Wow," DeeDee said. "Life is strange."

"That it is," Jake said.

They stayed up for another hour, putting the case together into a coherent format, then they wrote it all up in a Word document.

"I'll print it and take it to the cops right now," DeeDee said the moment they were done.

"No, don't," Jake said. "For one thing, neither one of us is in any condition to drive. We're too tired. For another, I've found it's always good to sleep on these things and not run off half-cocked. We very well may think of something in the morning that we haven't thought of now."

DeeDee sighed. "That's true, but at the moment all I'm feeling is wired. I don't know how I'm going to sleep tonight."

"You say that now," Jake said, "but if you take a long hot shower, I'm sure your body's need for sleep will kick in."

"You're probably right." DeeDee sighed. "I can't believe we've cracked it. I'm so happy for Tobias. This means there's no way they can charge him."

"Let's hope so," Jake said.

"Let's hope so?" DeeDee said, annoyed. "They can't. How could they possibly do that?"

Jake sighed. "This is not the time to be involved in a philosophical argument. Time to go to bed."

"You're right," DeeDee said. "To be honest, I'm not even thinking straight right now. That was some intensive investigation work we just did."

"That it was," Jake agreed.

And sure enough, after DeeDee had her shower, she began to feel drowsy, and she ended up sleeping with a towel wrapped around her, too tired to get up and put on her pajamas.

*****

The next morning, DeeDee was out of bed early even though she hadn't set her alarm clock. It was as if her body knew she had things to do. Jake was still asleep, so she quietly left him to enjoy his down time, while she went into the kitchen, fired up her laptop, and looked again at the document they'd written a few hours earlier.

It was almost surreal for her to read it with a fresh set of eyes. She thought back to the time she spoke with the culprit. She'd been looking into the eyes of a cold-blooded murderer, and hadn't even known it. Just thinking about it sent a shiver up her spine.

She cooked up a big breakfast of fried eggs, bacon, and muffins while she sipped her coffee. She thought about the day ahead as she watched the dogs devour their breakfasts. There was no doubt that it was going to be a dramatic day, to say the least.

DeeDee decided she'd go to the police station in Seattle and give them the document. Hopefully, they'd release Tobias Crank and arrest the real culprit. That evening she'd head to Canlis, where they were going to snag another murderer with the help of the FBI. If this was her life, she certainly never could have scripted what was happening. It sounded more like something she'd see on television or at the movies.

With all that had been going on, her catering business had taken a back seat. DeeDee wondered how Susie was doing with the marketing and the task of getting new clients, but she didn't want to call her quite yet. She decided it could wait until tomorrow once the two cases had been wrapped up.

But as it turned out, neither of the cases got wrapped up that day. Nothing happened as smoothly as DeeDee had imagined it would.

She had Jake check over the document again, and once they were both in agreement that it worked and their tired typos of the previous night had been fixed, she printed it out and headed to the Seattle police station.

When she got there a timid young female police officer was at the front desk. And Detective Kirton was standing right behind her, impatiently explaining to her how she was using the database in an inefficient way.

DeeDee gulped, holding the document she and Jake had made in her hand. She tried to make her voice sound confident and authoritative. "Detective Kirton," she said.

He looked up, annoyed at being interrupted during his scolding of the young policewoman. "What? Oh, you. Who are you again? You look vaguely familiar."

"I'm the caterer who did the event where Angel Bridges was murdered," DeeDee said. "And I know you have Tobias Crank in custody, but you've got the wrong person."

He crossed his arms and an amused smile flickered across his lips. Clearly, he was mocking her. "Oh, do I now?"

"Yes," DeeDee said firmly. "And this document proves it." She handed it to him and waited for him to read it. But he didn't read it. He slapped it down on the table and resumed his lecture to the young woman.

"Excuse me," DeeDee said. "It's extremely important that you read it now."

"As a matter of fact, it's not," he said, not even looking up. "You can go now."

"I'm not leaving until you read it," DeeDee said firmly. "Or are you going to arrest me for that? Just read it. It'll take you all of two minutes."

"You're like an annoying little fly, aren't you?" Detective Kirton said, but he did pick the paper up and began to read it. His eyes widened with shock, but then a nasty smile appeared on his lips. "Oh, this is all very Miss Marple, isn't it?"

"I don't know what you mean," DeeDee said, holding her chin up and glaring at him.

"You have no idea what you're doing," he said, taking the paper and crumpling it up into a ball. He threw it in the waste basket. "Stop wasting my time."

"But don't you think…"

"No, I don't think!" he began to shout. "Now, get out of here!"

DeeDee's hands were shaking with fury when she got back to her car, so much so it took her a moment or two to manage to get the key into the ignition. *How dare him speak to her like that!* She thought.

She was too enraged to drive to the ferry and worried she'd speed, so she parked on a side street. She slammed her hand on the top of the steering wheel, but she was too frustrated to stay in the car. She got out, and then realized she didn't have anywhere to go. She just needed to get the energy out her system.

But after a few more moments of being unable to calm down, she decided what she needed was a relaxing walk along the Sound with Yukon and Balto. She got in her car, drove to the ferry, and stewed the whole way going back home. She called Jake while she was on the ferry and ranted about what had happened.

"Okay," he said, sounding calm, which was always how he reacted to a crisis. "We'll have to work our way around it. We can do this, DeeDee. I know we can."

"Well, I'm glad you know it, because at the moment I certainly don't," she said, feeling too angry to be placated. "See you at home." She ended the call, and then went, "Arghhhh!"

That Detective Kirton guy was really good at getting under her skin, and he seemed to enjoy it. She knew that the evidence she'd presented him with was powerful. It defined a clear motive and a means. It was the result of many hours of frustration and dead ends.

How could he just throw it in the trash like he did?

But when she got home, Jake offered a quite soothing explanation. "There's a good chance he could make an arrest based on the evidence you gave him, but he doesn't want you to know that. It seems he's a guy with a huge ego. Probably just doesn't want to admit he got help from someone."

"Especially a mere caterer," DeeDee said bitterly, notwithstanding those were Laurence Powers' words rather than Detective Kirton's. She breathed out a stream of air.

"Maybe you're right. I hope so. At least then Tobias will be released and justice can be done. I need to go for a walk right now and release some of my frustration. I want to be calm, serene, and collected when we go to Canlis, and right now I'm feeling the exact opposite."

"Okay, darling," Jake said. "Try not to worry too much. These things have a way of working themselves out in the end. We'll come up with a plan. It'll be fine."

"All right," DeeDee said, not believing a word of it. She called to Yukon and Balto, put their leashes on them, and headed out for a walk. She tried to make Jake's words of comfort sink in. It worked, marginally. Nature and the great outdoors helped some, too.

At least, she didn't feel like punching the whole world into pieces when she came back, and the physical distance between Detective Kirton and her had given her a little perspective. "This might take time," she told Jake. "Just because it hasn't happened yet doesn't mean it's not going to happen."

"That's the spirit," Jake said. "I'm heading out for a planning meeting with Al and the guy from the FBI. Be back in a couple of hours."

"Okay," DeeDee said. "I need to catch up with Susie and see where we're at with getting new clients. Talking about marketing and such will help take my mind off of this case and cool me down. That way I'll be ready for tonight."

"Good idea," Jake said. "We need to be ready to leave at 6:00 this evening. With the time on the ferry, we'll be there exactly on time."

"Okay." DeeDee smiled. "I plan to luxuriate in the tub for far longer than necessary, and spend an inordinate amount of time on my hair and makeup. Why not?"

"I couldn't agree more. Why not?" Jake said. "Might as well add some champagne to the mix, and you'll have a truly enjoyable ritual."

"Nothing wrong with that." DeeDee said as she wrapped her arms around his neck and gave him a kiss on the cheek. "Not too much champagne, though. I'll need to be on my A-game, just in case anything goes wrong."

"I'm sure it won't," Jake said. "But I appreciate you keeping the drinking to a minimum. I'll be doing the same." He kissed her. "Bye, love. Enjoy the rest of your day."

"I plan to," DeeDee said. "If only to prove to myself that Detective Kirton can't get under my skin to the point my day is ruined."

Jake nodded. "I'm sure he'd be very pleased if he thought he could."

"Exactly," DeeDee said. "I refuse to give him the satisfaction."

Jake smiled at her as he left.

DeeDee spent a quiet afternoon with Susie, who suggested she come over to her house. DeeDee was ready for something to take her mind off of the Angel case, and soon, she was completely engrossed in the new marketing campaigns Susie was working on.

"We've had a few potential jobs come in," Susie said. "But I wanted to talk to you about them before we accepted any, and also… well, I'm waiting for some of the really high-end gourmet jobs to come in."

"Okay," DeeDee said. "Let's see what you've got."

Susie opened her emails and they picked through them, choosing which ones they wanted to take.

"I think gravitating more towards corporate clients will help, too," Susie said. "You know, slightly unusual business owners who buy their staff expensive gifts and take them on vacations. I'd like to get some employers like that. I think they'd like us to cater interesting experience dinners for their employees. But to do that, we really have to make a name for ourselves."

"I agree," DeeDee said. "At the same time, we don't want to restrict ourselves to the really over-the-top jobs, because we'll cut off a bunch of clients who just want sleek and elegant. Hey, what about having two arms of the business? One for the classic, one for the crazy."

Susie laughed. "Your choice. You want classic or crazy?"

DeeDee chuckled. "Okay, so the wording might need to be changed, but I think it would work."

All of the strategizing, thinking and planning helped to calm DeeDee down. Susie asked about the case, but DeeDee said they'd talk about it later, for now, she needed to think about other things.

She wanted to focus on the positive, too. At least by the end of the night, they'd have one case wrapped up.

But it didn't turn out like that at all.

In fact, it turned out much, much worse than her encounter with Detective Kirton.

No sooner had they walked into Canlis and taken their table, looking over at Al and the FBI guy in place, when everything was ruined. Joshua Jessup walked in and recognized the FBI agent. He pulled out a gun, fired twice, and fled. Al was down. The FBI guy was down. DeeDee felt like she couldn't breathe.

The Canlis restaurant was chaotic. People were screaming. The door was jammed with people trying to get out, falling all over each other. Some people had ducked under tables after the two gunshots rang out.

A waiter was standing over the bodies of Al and the FBI agent, frantically calling 9-1-1 on his cell. "A guy came in and shot two of our patrons!" he said. "They're laying here on the floor of the restaurant. One has blood coming from his arm, but he's conscious. The other one... I don't know..." The waiter's voice jumped. "He looks dead."

DeeDee and Jake heard all of this as they rushed over to the table where Al and the FBI agent had been sitting, hoping against hope it would be Al who was conscious and only bleeding from the arm.

But it wasn't.

Al was lying in a heap, his eyes closed.

Jake grabbed him and shook him hard. "Al! Al!" he shouted in his face. But there was no response.

CHAPTER EIGHTEEN

"He's not awake yet," the doctor said later that night. She'd come into the waiting room to talk to them. "But I feel very strongly that he will be very soon."

Cassie, who was at their apartment in Seattle, had rushed to the hospital, collapsed against DeeDee and cried with relief.

"He just got knocked out," the doctor continued. "Looks like his head hit something when he fell, because he's already got a big bruise. He has a pretty severe concussion caused by the bad fall he took. He also has a cracked rib and one heck of a bruise on his chest. But try not to worry. He's going to be fine and should be waking up soon."

"Thank goodness you made him wear a bulletproof vest, Cassie," Jake said.

The doctor nodded. "Thank goodness, indeed, or this would be a very different night for you."

"May I see him?" Cassie asked.

"Yes," the doctor said. "And feel free to ask for me anytime. I'm Dr. Sanchez, and Dr. Brookman will be taking over in the morning."

"Thank you," Cassie said, gratefully.

Dr. Sanchez motioned for a nurse to take them to Al's private room.

When they walked in, Cassie caught her breath. DeeDee looked at Jake and shook her head. What a mess. Al was hooked up to all kinds of wires and tubes and drips. His eyes were closed, and he didn't look good.

"He's really going to be fine?" Cassie asked, turning to the nurse.

"The doctor said he'll be absolutely fine," the nurse said. "There's no internal damage apart from the cracked rib, and that's far from fatal. I'll leave you alone with him for a while."

As soon as the nurse was gone, Cassie whirled around on Jake. "You guys... you're only to take infidelity cases from now on or... I don't know... neighbors spying on each other trying to work out who cut a hedge! I am not going through this ever again. I can't. It's too stressful."

"You're right," Jake said. "This..." He looked over at Al. "It's getting too serious now."

"You won't have to finish this case," DeeDee said. "Not with the FBI now being fully involved. Don't forget, this Jessup guy knows you were involved. I just hope nothing bad comes of it for us. You said this guy is dangerous."

"The FBI said they were offering protection for us," Jake said. "And surveillance. We gave fake addresses and names to Jessup, so I don't see how he can find us."

Cassie shook her head. "These types of people always know how to find someone. This ends here. Do you hear me?"

"I think you have a valid point," Jake said. "We'll take more pedestrian cases from now on."

"Good," Cassie said. "And if you want to expose yourself to all this danger, you're free to do so, but while Al is living with me, I want to be able to sleep at night. He'll have to move out if he insists on taking on any more cases like this."

In the past, DeeDee had found it all pretty exciting. Unlike Cassie, she liked the idea of catching criminals and making the world safer. But seeing Al lying in the hospital bed, motionless, with all the tubes sticking out of him, made her rethink it.

"I agree," she said quietly. "This can't go on."

They stayed by Al's bedside for a few minutes, but after a while, Cassie insisted that DeeDee and Jake go home. "Get your sleep," she said. "I want to be here when he wakes up, but who knows when that could be? I know you have the Angel Bridges investigation to work on as well, so go. Al knows you care. I know you care. I'll be in touch as soon as I can."

"Do you want us to get some things from your apartment?" DeeDee asked. "Your clothes, toothbrush, snacks, things like that?"

"Oh, yes, thank you. I hadn't even thought of that. Please, if it's not too much trouble."

"Too much trouble?" DeeDee said, incredulous. "Are you kidding? We'd be glad to."

Cassie smiled, gave them the apartment key, and told them the alarm code.

DeeDee and Jake took a cab to Cassie and Al's apartment, still in their evening wear. They held each other's hand tightly and didn't say much. DeeDee packed up some clothes for Cassie and Al, while Jake stayed in the kitchen, fixing snacks and drinks to take along. DeeDee jumped at every strange sound she heard.

Could some hitman hired by Joshua Jessup possibly be stalking the corridors of the apartment building, gun in hand, ready to pounce on them and blow their brains out? The question haunted her the whole time she organized the overnight bags, and made her hurry, not folding things as neatly as she normally would have. But she was sure neither Cassie nor Al would care.

They went back to the hospital, still in evening wear, then took their car to the ferry, lucky to catch the last one of the night to Bainbridge Island. By the time they got home, they didn't even have enough energy to shower. They zombie-walked into their bedroom, changed clothes, let the dogs out, and collapsed on the bed, falling asleep instantly.

The next morning, DeeDee was the first to wake up. She leaned over and shook Jake awake. "As far as we know, Tobias Crank is still in jail for a crime he didn't commit. If Detective Kirton won't follow up our evidence and take action on it, we have to."

Jake, bleary eyed, stretched and sat up. His voice was slurred with sleep. "What's our plan, DeeDee?"

"We gather everyone together in the theater. Ooh, actually, if I remember correctly, there's a matinee today. Let me check." She grabbed her purse from the nightstand, and pulled out her phone. It only had two percent of its battery left, but that was enough. She quickly searched for the opera website.

"This is perfect!" she said. "We'll gather the players together before the matinee and reveal what we've learned in front of everyone. Hopefully with that kind of pressure, they'll admit it. We can record the confession, and then that should be enough to persuade Detective Kirton. He can't turn his back on that kind of evidence."

"There's no guarantee we'll get the confession, but it's worth a try," Jake said. "Let's do it. But how are we going to get them all together before the matinee begins?"

"I know Tobias Crank gets the whole cast and crew together before a performance and gives them a pep talk."

Jake smiled. "That must be a sight to see."

"I'm just hoping the replacement director does the same thing."

A few hours later, they found that, yes, that was the case. Jake hung around in the lobby a couple of hours before the show was due to start, looking for any sign of the very slim, dark haired assistant director.

DeeDee was able to get into the theater behind a lighting man, who thankfully didn't ask any questions. She stood to the side inconspicuously, waiting to see if anyone turned up.

The assistant director, as DeeDee suspected, arrived from backstage, rather than the front of the house, so DeeDee quickly texted Jake. She ran to the door and held it open for him, at the same time keeping an eye on the stage, where the cast began appearing in dribs and drabs, sitting on the chairs arranged in a circle on stage. DeeDee was also keeping an eye open for their suspect.

"Yes," she said under her breath, when their suspect arrived on the stage with the other players and took a seat in one of the chairs.

After Jake arrived, DeeDee closed the door behind him. They looked at each other, DeeDee set her charged phone to record mode, and they briskly strode onto the stage.

"Hold everything!" Jake yelled. "We know who killed Angel Bridges!"

DeeDee expected the assistant director to be annoyed by their interruption, but she wasn't. She didn't even question why they were there. She turned to them and said, "Really?"

"Yes," DeeDee said, as they walked to the center of the stage and stood in front of the players who were seated in the chairs. She looked around at the cast and crew, careful to not let her eyes rest on anyone in particular. "And that person is sitting right here on this stage. Now, this is your last chance to tell the truth, before we expose you. Do you want to take this opportunity?"

She left a long pause.

Laurence Powers stood up, and everyone gasped.

He waved his hand at them, annoyed. "Oh, do shut up," he said in his posh English accent. "I'm not admitting to killing anyone, because I didn't. I'm just inquiring as to whether this whole process is legal. Who are these people? This seems highly suspicious."

"This is DeeDee, the caterer from the opening night event at Tobias'. I don't know who the gentleman is. But in any case, you shouldn't question it. It only makes you look guilty, Laurence," Siobhan said.

DeeDee looked at Jake, and then spoke. "So is that your strategy, Siobhan? To go along with everything sweetly to hide the fact that you snuck out of dinner that night, put poison in a champagne glass, and gave it to Angel Bridges, with the intention to kill, which it did."

"What?" Siobhan looked genuinely overwhelmed. "No! I swear I didn't!"

"Who looks guilty now, Siobhan?" Laurence taunted. "How ironic."

"But why?" the assistant director said. "What possible motive could she have had?"

"It's a sad story," DeeDee said. "Siobhan's daughter Marina was on the road to becoming a successful actress. I discovered online that Marina spiraled into heroin addiction when she didn't get a part she wanted, and then finally died of an overdose.

"It was a part she was in the final reading for, and later it was suspected that the actress who got the part had slept with the director and had also given Marina false information about the director, so she'd make a faux pas at a grand dinner they had.

"I read it all on a gossip website. It didn't name the movie. But I worked out the dates and the details, and they correlate with Angel Bridges' breakout movie, *A Dance at Sunset.*"

She turned to Siobhan. "You, Siobhan, killed Angel Bridges, because she became a star, and your daughter is dead. You thought your daughter should have been the star, so you killed Angel Bridges in cold blood, since you believed she 'took' your daughter from you."

Siobhan was deathly pale. "I didn't. Really, I didn't. All of that is true. Angel did get the part instead of Marina. And Marina did die as a result of heroin addiction. But I didn't kill Angel."

"You did!" DeeDee said to her in an accusing tone of voice, not quite sure what else she could say.

Siobhan stood up and spoke desperately. "I didn't, DeeDee! You must believe me! I can see why it looks bad, I can. But honestly, I had nothing to do with Angel's death."

DeeDee watched her carefully, her heart feeling like it would tear in two at any moment. She didn't know what to believe.

As she was trying to form a response, Lola Newman burst into tears. "She didn't do it!" She wiped tears from her cheek. "I can attest to that. Because I know who did do it."

CHAPTER NINETEEN

Lola continued to cry, so much so that when everyone kept asking her who did it, she couldn't spit out the words. DeeDee was fully expecting her to say that she did it, so she could play the part of Nefertiti. She tried not to let herself feel too confused, given what was happening. She hadn't expected this at all. She breathed in and out deeply, trying to center herself.

"It was Laurence Powers," Lola finally said.

Everyone gasped.

"The night of the murder, I left the dining room to go to the bathroom. I saw him coming from the balcony where Angel was on the phone with her husband, and then just a few moments later, she was dead. I was nearby when someone found her body."

"So," DeeDee said. "Laurence, is this true?"

Laurence looked at Lola for a long moment.

"It is," Lola said. "I'd be willing to testify to it before a jury. I'd swear on the Bible and tell them what I saw."

Laurence dropped his head. "It is true. It is. But I was incredibly drunk. I can't be held responsible for my actions."

DeeDee wanted to leave no room for doubt on the recording. "So, you, Laurence Powers, are saying that you murdered Angel Bridges by putting poison in her drink and giving it to her on the balcony, causing her to die?"

Laurence looked up at her, a defeated man. "Yes." He looked almost relieved, like he'd been waiting for the truth to come out.

"But… why?" Siobhan said, on the brink of tears. "What possible reason could you have to kill her?"

"I'll come clean," Laurence said. "Angel and I were having an affair. Our constant arguing in rehearsals was an act we decided to put on, to ensure that our affair wasn't discovered. She told me that she was going to leave her husband, and had already initiated talks about a divorce.

"But when I saw her leave the table when she got a call, I was suspicious, so I followed her. And then I heard what I feared the most. She was talking to her husband, telling him she loved him. It was then that I decided to kill her."

Everyone was in shock.

"But that hardly follows the profile of a crime of passion," Jake said. "Strangling, pushing her off the balcony, or grabbing a knife and stabbing her to death would be what you'd expect. Why poison? And where did you get it from? The way you talk about the killing, it sounds like it was spur of the moment. But poison is not a spur of the moment weapon, Mr. Powers. That shows premeditation."

Laurence was silent for a long time, looking down at the floor. He finally said, "Fine. I haven't been truthful with you. I said it like that so it would be judged as a crime of passion, and I'd get a lesser sentence than something premeditated. The truth is I already knew she'd lied to me about her husband.

"I tried to talk to her about it, but she kept lying and lying to me. And I decided, if I can't have her all to myself, nobody can, so I decided to kill her. The poison wasn't hard to find. I ordered it online."

"That's sick!" Siobhan said. "You killed her, just because she wouldn't leave her husband for you?"

"That I did," he said. "I've been regretting it ever since. I am happy to hand myself over to the police and face whatever consequences come my way."

DeeDee called the police station. "Detective Kirton, please," she said. "It's urgent. We have the killer of Angel Bridges here, he's confessed, and we need him to come to the opera house and arrest him.

"Okay, just a sec, I'm going to put you on hold."

"Fine," DeeDee said. "Just hurry, please."

The woman soon came back on the line. "He told me to tell you, 'no, thank you'."

"Huh?"

"I can't say any more than that," the woman said. "That's the message he told me to pass on."

"No, thank you!" DeeDee said, enraged. "I tell him we have a murderer, here, with a recorded confession, and he says no, thank you?"

"I'm sorry, ma'am," the woman said.

"You don't sound very sorry," DeeDee said. "Otherwise you'd have given me some other option to take." She pressed end call furiously. "Fine," she said. "Laurence, you're going to have to come with us in a cab. And don't you dare try to escape."

"I'll come along with you," Siobhan said, "to make sure he

doesn't. Three pairs of hands are better than two."

"Thank you," DeeDee said.

"I can assure you it will not be necessary," Laurence Powers said. "I am no more likely to try to abscond than I am to grow two heads."

Nevertheless, the three of them, DeeDee, Jake, and Siobhan, escorted Laurence out the theater. They wished they had handcuffs, but of course they didn't, so they made a makeshift version from some rope one of the crew found backstage.

A cab was there in a matter of moments, and soon they were on their way to the police station. There was terrible traffic, and Laurence was sitting quite still between Jake and DeeDee, with Siobhan in front of him, facing backward. The doors were locked. Consequently, DeeDee's mind relaxed a little, and she started to look back on the events that had occurred over the past couple of weeks with a fresh perspective, knowing Laurence was the killer.

Then something dawned on her.

"Hang on a minute! Lola said she left the dining room and saw Laurence, but I'm sure Tanya said Lola didn't leave the table at all!"

"Who's Tanya?" Siobhan asked.

"One of the wait staff," Jake explained.

"I can't be sure, though…" DeeDee's mind was whirring like crazy. Is that what Tanya had said? Or had she remembered it wrong? She didn't even have Tanya's number, Susie did. Susie would remember! She quickly fished her phone out of her purse and called her. "Susie!"

"Hi, DeeDee. Are you okay?"

"Did Tanya say that Lola left the dinner table, or didn't leave it?"

"Who's Lola again?"

"The glamorous young woman with all the hair."

"Yes. She said she knew she didn't leave the table, because she remembered how much she was flirting with some of the men at the table."

"Oh!" DeeDee said. "Thank you so much, we'll talk later." She ended the call. "Lola was lying. So how did she know you did it, Laurence?"

He stayed calm and answered evenly, "Heaven knows. Psychic intuition, perhaps?"

"I know you don't believe in any of that," DeeDee said. "Tell me, what's going on?"

"Nothing," he said tersely. "I've told you everything already. Aren't you happy now?"

"No," DeeDee said. "There's something you're not telling me."

"Was Lola somehow involved, Laurence?" Siobhan asked.

"No."

"I don't believe you," DeeDee said. She gestured to the cab driver. "Take us back to the opera house, please. Turn around!"

"You're off on a wild goose chase," Laurence said haughtily.

And it turned out he was right. DeeDee left Laurence in the cab with Jake and Siobhan, and ran into the opera house. She went straight into the theater, which was now empty, then ran onto the stage and into the wings, trying to find her way backstage.

She came across a stage hand. "Where's Lola Newman?"

"I... I don't know," the stagehand said, bewildered. "In her dressing room, I guess?"

"Where is it?"

"Her name is on the door," he said. "You'll find it."

DeeDee ran through to the backstage corridor, where there were a few people milling around. She ran down the hallway, looking at every single door, checking the names. Then, finally, she came upon it. Lola Newman.

But when she tried the door, it was locked. "Lola!" she yelled. "Lola!" There was no answer.

She looked toward the end of the corridor, where a group of stage management crew, recognizable by their black clothing, was gathered. "Who has the master key?" she asked urgently. "I need to open this door now! Hurry!"

After what felt like an eternity, but was really only five minutes, someone came along with a master key, and opened the door. When it swung open, it was just as DeeDee had feared.

CHAPTER TWENTY

Lola's dressing room was completely empty. The window was open, the curtain flapping in the breeze.

"She's gone," DeeDee said.

Even so, she went into the bathroom to see if Lola was hiding in there. She looked in ridiculous places that were too small for a person to hide in, but that's how desperate she was.

"Man," she said, slamming the heel of her hand against the bathroom counter. She decided to return to where Jake and Siobhan were waiting in the taxi so they could escort Laurence to the police station. Lola would have to wait.

But when she got outside and looked for the cab, it was gone. "What?" she said, her heart beating at what seemed like a million miles per hour. She looked left and right, and at all the people on the sidewalk. But none of them was Laurence, or Jake, or Siobhan.

"What the...?" DeeDee, after a moment of shock, got out her phone and called Jake. He didn't answer the first time, so she called again.

When he answered, he was breathing heavily, panting from running. "I... lost... him..."

"What?"

"He was loosening the ropes behind his back the whole time, DeeDee," Jake said, trying to catch a breath. "Almost as soon as you left the taxi, so did he. And Siobhan and I have been running, trying to catch him. She couldn't keep up with us, and now I've lost him. I'm so, so sorry, DeeDee. I've ruined your investigation."

"No, you haven't," she said. "We'll find him, don't worry. We have to call the cops."

"They won't be any use," he said, sounding on the brink of tears, which was very rare for him.

"We'll go to someone else," she said. "Not Detective Kirton. But for now, I want to go to Lola's hotel room, just in case she's there."

"She's gone, too?"

"Yes. You can meet me there, if you want, I'm going to run there. In all this traffic, it'll be quicker than getting a cab."

"Okay," he said. "Which hotel?"

She told him the hotel name and the room number, and after a quick run, pushing past pedestrians, she finally got there. She didn't wait for Jake, she just ran inside, explained why she was there, and thankfully was allowed to take the elevator to the floor where Lola's room was located.

When DeeDee got to her room, the door was open. She stepped partially into the room, only to find Lola and Laurence together, frantically throwing things in small travel bags. DeeDee gasped.

Lola saw her and ran into the bathroom. There was a crash, and two seconds later, Lola returned, a broken bottle in her hand. She rushed at DeeDee and blocked her path to the door.

"If you scream," Lola said, "I'll rip your throat apart with this. I want you to step completely inside the room, and then I'll close the door behind you."

DeeDee weighed her odds. Could she somehow push Lola's arm away and make a safe getaway? Or would she get slashed in the process? She decided to play it safe, and edged into the room. Lola closed the door and locked it.

"Good girl," Laurence said, his eyes glinting nastily.

"The two of you killed her together, didn't you?" DeeDee said. "Lola was the planner, and Laurence executed the plan." A wave of nausea churned through her stomach. "Was this all so you could get the part of Nefertiti?"

"She was acting above her station in every way," Laurence spat. "A movie actress, thinking she could take on the opera world. I hated her and so did Lola. She wanted her out the way, and I was more than happy to oblige. Now, we're going to go someplace else, together."

"What I don't understand is why you admitted to killing her," DeeDee said.

"Easy. I knew you'd be so complacent you'd found the murderer, that I could get away from you. I trusted that Lola would get away from the theater and we could meet here, which, as you can see, we did."

Lola nuzzled into him, and DeeDee felt sick. "We're lovers," Lola crowed.

"And you could very easily meet a sticky end, too, so don't even think about trying to escape. Just one accidental trip, and you could go flying over the balcony," Laurence said as he motioned towards the open sliding glass door that led to the balcony.

DeeDee swallowed. "Please don't kill me. I still have one more question," she said quietly.

"What is that?" Laurence asked.

"Were you really having an affair with Angel?"

Laurence and Lola laughed. "In the beginning I was enamored of her, but once I met Lola, I knew I was really in love, but I couldn't end it outright. I pretended with Angel, because Lola and I knew what we were going to do. We didn't want anything to get in our way, particularly a suspicious diva."

He looked at Lola with loving eyes. "Lola is the love of my life. Angel was a stage dalliance, nothing more…"

"Enough, Laurence. DeeDee, we won't kill you," Lola interrupted. "But we're going to tie you up, so you can't run to the pigs and tell on us. You'll be here for a long, long time, because I'm going to put the Do Not Disturb sign on the door. Who knows, you might even starve to death by then." She laughed. "The room is booked for months and months, so it's not like they'll come check up on it."

Just then, the door burst open. Jake ran into the room, followed by several hotel employees.

Lola was caught so off-guard that her broken bottle weapon was of no use. Jake charged at her, and it flew out of her hand and crashed on the carpet. The hotel employees piled onto Lola and Laurence, until neither of them could move.

Jake ran to DeeDee and wrapped his arms around her. "I stayed outside the room and heard what was going on. I tried to open the door, but it was locked. I rushed downstairs and got the hotel employees to give me a key to unlock the door."

"Oh, Jake," she said, barely able to catch a breath, "I was so scared. I thought for sure they were going to kill me.

One of the hotel employees was on the phone to the police.

"They'll definitely come this time," DeeDee said.

And they did. The hotel employees were very kind, trying to take care of DeeDee and Jake as best they could. They settled them in the lounge by the bar, with complementary drinks. DeeDee ordered a gin and tonic. "With a lot of gin," she said.

They didn't have enough energy to speak, so they simply watched as the police arrived, headed by Detective Kirton, and then watched again as the police left with Lola and Laurence in handcuffs.

Lola caught sight of DeeDee and Jake and swore loudly at them.

This caught Detective Kirton's attention, and he looked over in their direction. To DeeDee's shock, he nodded at them with respect, as if to say, "Thank you."

DeeDee managed to laugh shakily. "I expect that's all the thanks we're going to get from him."

EPILOGUE

What DeeDee had said was true. There was no further thank you from the police department or Detective Kirton. They were called to testify, though, and DeeDee's recording in the opera house was used as evidence in the trial.

She hadn't managed to get a recording of the incident in the hotel room, since she'd been caught so off guard, but it didn't matter. There was still enough evidence to make the case against Lola and Laurence.

Although thanks from the police department was not forthcoming, it was very forthcoming from Tobias Crank and his generous benefactor, Lowell Marks.

Everyone who had been involved in solving the case, DeeDee, Jake, Al, Cassie, Susie, Tanya, and Siobhan, were invited for an all-expenses paid weekend trip to New York, where Lowell Marks lived.

It turned out he lived in a penthouse in one of New York's most expensive buildings. His home was a wonder of expensive art and voice-activated technology. It was like stepping into another world.

When it was time for dinner, he sat at the head of a long, polished black table and raised a glass of expensive champagne.

"I invited all of you here to personally thank you for working so hard to solve the case of Angel Bridges' murder," he said. "I have discovered from Tobias that the police were worse than useless, and in fact even accused the wrong people."

He turned to DeeDee and the rest of them. "Thankfully, some very kind, smart and noble people stepped up to the plate and did what the police could not, or would not, do.

"DeeDee Wilson, a stellar caterer, was even confronted by the two miscreants as she attempted to seek justice for Angel Bridges. I think this deserves extra compensation." He drew an envelope out of his pocket and gave it to DeeDee.

"Please accept this as a token of our gratitude. Because of you, Tobias Crank, our illustrious director, is a free man. Free to continue working his other-worldly magic. This is not only a victory for us individually, it is a victory for truth, justice, and art.

"In the opera, we see the Fates tear men and women's lives apart, but we also see their great benevolence at times. We know not the mysterious forces that move humanity and the machinations of the world that encircle humanity. Invisible forces, unknowable forces. But we can safely say today that although the Fates briefly dealt us a blow, they then more than compensated us for the trouble they put us through.

"Let this be a lesson to all of us. A lesson that no matter how bad things get, we will always hold out hope. Hope in ourselves, hope in the universal scales that keep things in balance. Those with noble intentions are always rewarded. And I only ask that we may keep those noble intentions in sight as we move through this mystery called life, so the Fates may smile upon us, if not always, then at least, in the end.

"To a noble life!" he said, raising his glass.

"To a noble life!" everyone echoed, clinking their glasses against each other's.

"Now, enough of that mumbo jumbo!" Lowell Marks said. "Let's eat!"

Jake leaned into DeeDee and whispered in her ear. "I can see why Lowell Marks and Tobias Crank get along so well together."

"Me too," DeeDee said with a grin.

After dinner was over, they all retired to the grand drawing room, which had a double-high ceiling with an upstairs mezzanine.

In a quiet corner, DeeDee and Jake huddled together, and DeeDee opened the envelope Lowell Marks had given her. Her mouth dropped open.

She showed it to Jake, and his mouth dropped open, too.

Inside was a check made out for no less than half a million dollars.

"My, my, my," DeeDee said. "Doesn't life bring unexpected twists and turns?"

Jake smiled, still in wonderment. "Indeed it does."

RECIPES

THAI CRAB SALAD

Ingredients:
1 cup rice vinegar
¼ cup + 1 tbsp. sugar
2 garlic cloves, minced
2 Thai red chiles, minced
3 carrots, thinly sliced
¼ cup fresh lime juice
¼ cup fresh tangerine juice
1 shallot, minced
2 tbsp. Asian fish sauce
1/3 cup water
2 large green mangos, peeled and finely sliced
2 seedless cucumbers, peeled and finely sliced
2 bunches watercress, thick stems discarded and then chopped
½ cup shredded basil leaves
1/3 cup coarsely chopped mint
1/3 cup coarsely chopped cilantro
1 lb. lump crab
3 scallions, green parts only, thinly sliced
OPTIONAL: ½ tsp. sambal oelek chili paste or other Asian hot sauce

Directions:

In a medium bowl combine the vinegar with ¼ cup of the sugar and half of the garlic and chiles. Add the carrots and let stand at room temperature for 1 hour.

In a medium bowl combine the lime and tangerine juices, shallots, fish sauce, sambal oelek and water. Stir in the remaining garlic, chiles, and 1 tbsp. sugar.

In a large bowl combine the mangos, cucumbers, watercress, basil, mint, and cilantro. Drain the carrots, shaking off excess liquid, and add them to the bowl. Add the juice mixture and toss well. Plate the salad and mound the crab on top. Garnish with the scallions and serve.

PEANUT BUTTER AND LAMB SOUP

Ingredients:
1 lb. lamb shoulder, cut into pieces
1 tbsp. olive oil
2 onions, chopped
1 jalapeno pepper, finely chopped
1 sweet potato, chopped
½ cup peanut butter
4 garlic cloves, minced
2 tsp. turmeric
2 tsp. paprika
2 tsp. cumin
15 oz. can crushed tomatoes
1 can water
Salt and freshly ground pepper to taste

Directions:

Heat a soup pot on medium high heat. Add the lamb and sear on all sides. Remove from pot. Add olive oil to pot and reduce heat to medium. Add onion and jalapeno pepper. Sauté for 4 minutes. Add garlic, paprika, turmeric, and cumin. Sauté for 1 minute.

Return lamb to pot. Add crushed tomatoes, water, peanut butter, and sweet potato to pot. Turn heat to high and bring to a boil. Lower heat and simmer for 1 hour. Add more water if desired. Ladle into bowls and serve.

NOTE: This is very good served over rice.

OLIVE OIL CAKE

Ingredients:
1 ½ cups olive oil + more for oiling pans
1 cup fresh orange juice
1 tsp. sea salt
2 cups all-purpose flour
½ tsp. baking soda
½ tsp. baking powder
3 large eggs, room temperature
2 cups granulated sugar
1 ¼ cups whole milk
¼ cups orange liqueur, dark rum, or whisky
1 tbsp. lemon zest, grated
1 tsp. anise seeds (If these are unavailable, substitute fennel or caraway seeds.)
2 tsp. rosemary, finely chopped + 2 sprigs for garnish
6 tbsp. lemon or orange marmalade

Directions:
Preheat oven to 350 degrees. Oil two 10" round cake pans with olive oil. Pour the orange juice into a small saucepan. Bring to a simmer over medium heat and cook until reduced to ¼ cup. Remove from heat, stir in salt, and let cool to room temperature.

In a bowl sift together the flour, baking soda, and baking powder. Set aside. In a stand mixer fitted with the paddle attachment, beat the eggs on medium until blended. Add sugar, olive oil, milk, liqueur, lemon zest, anise seeds or substitute, and 1 tsp. of rosemary. Mix on medium speed until well blended. Add the flour mixture and mix until blended.

Divide the batter evenly between the prepared cake pans. Place in the oven and bake until a toothpick inserted in the center comes out clean, about 1 hour. Remove from oven. Place on cooking racks and cool to room temperature.

Run a knife blade around the inside edge of each pan to loosen the sides of the cake. Turn the cakes out of the pan, then turn upright and place on flat serving plates. Using an icing spatula spread 3 tbsp. of marmalade over the top of each cake. Sprinkle the remaining 1 tsp. rosemary evenly over the cakes, dividing it evenly. Garnish the center of each cake with a rosemary sprig. Slice, serve, and enjoy!

TOMATO CARPACCIO WITH ARUGULA & HERBS

Ingredients:
Vinaigrette:
2 tbsp. fresh lemon juice
1 tbsp. minced shallot
1 tsp. minced garlic
½ cup extra-virgin olive oil
3 cups diced red and/or yellow tomatoes, diced
1 tbsp. tarragon, finely chopped
1 tbsp. flat leaf parsley, finely chopped
1 tbsp. chives, finely chopped
3 tbsp. basil, finely chopped
Sea salt and freshly ground pepper, to taste
4 large red and/or yellow tomatoes
6 oz. baby arugula
3 oz. wedge Parmesan cheese

Directions:
To make the vinaigrette, in a bowl stir together the lemon juice, shallot, and garlic. Slowly whisk in the olive oil and emulsify. Add the remaining vinaigrette ingredients, including the salt and pepper to taste. Mix well.

Cut each tomato in ¼" thick slices. On a round platter, arrange the slices by slightly overlapping them and alternating colors if using both red and yellow.

Spoon half the vinaigrette over the sliced tomatoes. In a bowl toss the arugula with the remaining vinaigrette. Place the arugula in the center of the tomato-covered platter. Shave thin slices of Parmesan over the platter. Serve and enjoy!

SHRIMP STUFFED PASTA SHELLS

Ingredients:
12 oz. box jumbo pasta shells
½ cup + 3 tbsp. extra-virgin olive oil
2 lbs. rock shrimp, deveined and shells removed
3 tbsp. garlic, finely sliced
2 tsp. fennel seeds
2 cups dry white wine
28 oz. tomato purée
2 tbsp. basil, finely chopped
2 tsp. tarragon, finely chopped
¼ cup fine dry bread crumbs
2 tbsp. freshly grated Parmesan cheese
OPTIONAL: ¼ cup Pernod or brandy

Directions:
Cook pasta according to package directions until ¾ done, about 10 minutes. Drain in a colander and rinse with cool water to stop cooking. Drain thoroughly and transfer to a wide, shallow bowl. Toss with 2 tbsp. olive oil, coating the shells evenly. Preheat oven to 350 degrees.

In a large skillet, heat ¼ cup olive oil over high heat. When oil begins to smoke, add shrimp, spreading in a single layer. Cook for 1 minute, then turn and cook for 1 more minute. Let cool.

Return skillet to high heat and add 2 tbsp. olive oil. Add the garlic. If using Pernod add and step back, because it will probably flame up. Add the wine.

Add tomato purée and cook uncovered over medium heat until the liquid is reduced by half, 20 – 25 minutes. Season to taste with salt and pepper.

Return the shrimp to the skillet and cook for 15 seconds. Remove the pan from the heat and using a slotted spoon, transfer the shrimp to a food processor. Process the shrimp for 15 seconds. Add 6 tbsp. of the tomato broth to the shrimp.

Combine the parsley, basil, and tarragon in a small bowl. Add half of the herb mixture to the shrimp and half to the broth remaining in the pan. Add the bread crumbs and cheese to the shrimp. Pulse to combine the ingredients.

Using a large spoon, fill the pasta shells with the shrimp mixture and place them, shell opening facing up, in an oiled 9" x 13" baking dish. Drizzle the remaining ¼ cup olive oil over the top of the shells. Cover with aluminium foil. Bake the shells in the preheated oven for 20 minutes. Place the skillet with the tomato broth in it over medium heat.

Arrange the baked pasta shells on a large deep platter. Pour the tomato sauce over the pasta shells. Serve and enjoy!

LEAVE A REVIEW

I'd really appreciate it you could take a few seconds and leave a review of The Final Curtain Call.

Just go to the link below. Thank you so much, it means a lot to me ~ Dianne

http://getbook.at/TFCC

Paperbacks & Ebooks for FREE

Go to www.dianneharman.com/freepaperback.html and get your FREE copies of Dianne's books and favorite recipes immediately by signing up for her newsletter.

Once you've signed up for her newsletter you're eligible to win three paperbacks. One lucky winner is picked every week. Hurry before the offer ends!

ABOUT THE AUTHOR

Dianne lives in Huntington Beach, California, with her husband, Tom, a former California State Senator, and her boxer dog, Kelly. Her passions are cooking, reading, and dogs, so whenever she has a little free time, you can either find her in the kitchen, playing with Kelly in the back yard, or curled up with the latest book she's reading. Her award winning books include:

Cedar Bay Cozy Mystery Series

Cedar Bay Cozy Mystery Series - Boxed Set

Liz Lucas Cozy Mystery Series

Liz Lucas Cozy Mystery Series - Boxed Set

High Desert Cozy Mystery Series

High Desert Cozy Mystery Series - Boxed Set

Northwest Cozy Mystery Series

Northwest Cozy Mystery Series - Boxed Set

Midwest Cozy Mystery Series

Midwest Cozy Mystery Series - Boxed Set

Jack Trout Cozy Mystery Series

Cottonwood Springs Cozy Mystery Series

Cottonwood Springs Mystery Series – Boxed Set

Coyote Series

Midlife Journey Series, Midlife Journey Boxed Set

Red Zero Series, Black Dot Series

The Holly Lewis Mystery Series, Holly Lewis Boxed Set

Newsletter

If you would like to be notified of her latest releases please go to www.dianneharman.com and sign up for her newsletter.

Website: www.dianneharman.com,
Blog: www.dianneharman.com/blog
Email: dianne@dianneharman.com

PUBLISHING 10/30/19

HOLLY AND THE MISSING DOG

BOOK FOUR OF

THE HOLLY LEWIS MYSTERY SERIES

http://getbook.at/HMD

A missing dog.

A heartbroken young man.

Stolen out of anger or affection?

Or to be put at stud?

After all, the Shar-Pei was a beauty and worth a lot of money!

When Wade's dog goes missing, Holly and the sheriff's department join in the search. But is it too late for Zeus?

If you've ever felt the pain of losing a dog, you'll have no trouble identifying with Holly's boyfriend as he searches for his best friend.

This is the fourth book in the Holly Lewis Mystery Series, a modern-day version of Nancy Drew by a two-time USA Today Bestselling Author.

Open your smartphone, point and shoot at the QR code below. You will be taken to Amazon where you can pre-order 'Holly and the Food Pantry'.

(Download the QR code app onto your smartphone from the iTunes or Google Play store in order to read the QR code below.)

Printed in Great Britain
by Amazon

51094344R00108